DONOVAN

A MONEY, POWER & SEX NOVELLA

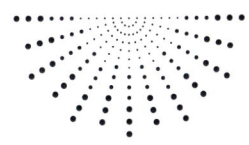

NORIAN LOVE

This is a work of fiction. Names, characters, businesses, organizations, places, events, and incidents either are the product of the author's imagination or used factiously. Any resemblance to actual persons, living or dead, events or locales is entirely coincidental.

Copyright

© 2022 by Norian Love

© 2022 Project 7even Publishing

ISBN-13: 978-1-7366707-4-3

ISBN-10: 1-7366707-4-3

No part of this book may be reproduced in any form or by any electronic or mechanical means, including information storage and retrieval systems, without written permission from the author, except for the use of brief quotations in a book review.

All rights reserved.

www.norianlove.com

To Houston, with love
-Norian

ACKNOWLEDGMENTS

To those of you who have taken the time to walk with me on these little personal journeys before each book, thank you. I'm so grateful to each and every one of you for this quality time we share. I want you to know how much I value your support and I'm glad you're here with me in this season of my life

This book in many ways is a homecoming; equal parts an ode to the city of Houston and a return to the Money, Power & Sex series. To the former, you're my home. We didn't always get along but we've watched each other grow. Through all of my travels, Houston is the place I will always champion and protect. I'm sorry that I didn't realize that sooner. To the latter, I've missed all of these characters and it seems like right now they have an abundance of things to share. I hope I share your stories well.

There are so many people to thank for this journey. As always, I thank my family for always being supportive of me. I love you all without measure. Thanks to my Project 7 family, I can't believe how much we've grown. Special thank you to my Admin for oftentimes laying down the law and the tireless man hours helping me birth these projects.

I hope you enjoy this prequel. For those of you who are starting with this book, I can't wait to hear your views on it. I'm very active on social media, so never fail to hit me up at @norianlove on all platforms.

With Love,
   Norian

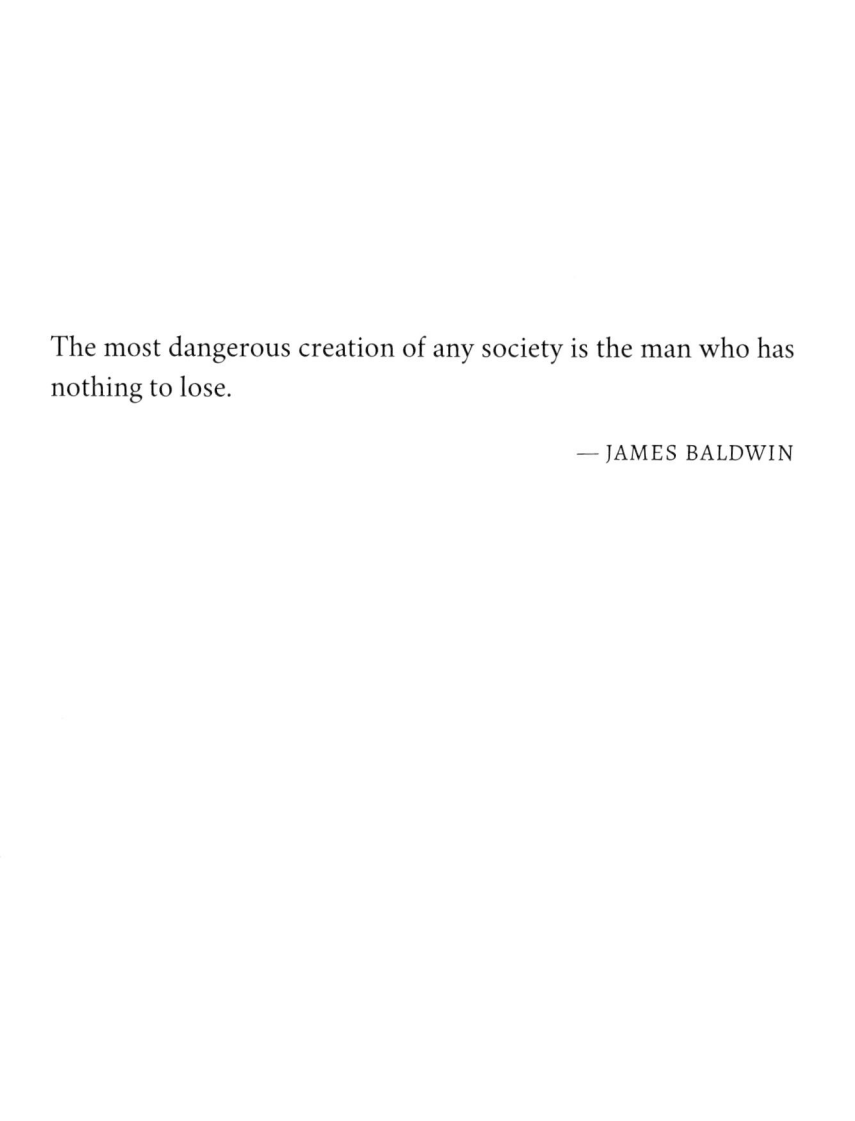

The most dangerous creation of any society is the man who has nothing to lose.

— JAMES BALDWIN

1
WELCOME 2 HOUSTON

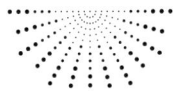

"This club is dope." Carlos said to Donovan as he scanned the room. The ambiance in Club Indigo was appealing from the oblong glasses they served the drinks in, to the all-female staff who worked at the club.

Donovan turned to Carlos and said, "Where is the man of the hour?"

He said nothing as he watched Carlos try to scan for him in a sea of people, to no avail. After a spell, Donovan then turned to his best friend Rico and asked,

"Rosey, where's the man of the hour?"

"Top left corner in VIP; just took his 4th shot of tequila. Looks like they are switching out waitresses though, because the last one kept getting cussed out by a couple of guys in the entourage from what I can tell from here." Surprised by the response, Carlos turned to Rico and asked.

"How in the hell did you just do that? You've been talking with me all night, drinking and dancing with women."

Unsurprised by the response, Donovan turned back to Carlos,

leaned in and said, "See, in this game we're in, you can only have one focus. You gotta be a wolf. Sometimes you're with the pack, sometimes you're alone, but no matter what, you're always on the hunt, you feel me? Friends, pussy, feelings are all secondary to the hunt. Every move we make in this thing of ours could mean freedom or jail. Life or death. Ain't no feelings in this game. We gotta be cold and calculative, and every move has to mean something." He watched as Terrance, Rico, and Carlos all processed what he was saying differently. Nerves of steel were going to be needed for what they were about to do, so he figured one last pep talk couldn't hurt.

"Like wolves?" Carlos asked.

"Just like wolves," Donovan replied as he scanned the area and took a drag of his Camel cigarette. He exhaled the smoke with a dragon's exhaust and continued.

"See, most people get tripped up because they get emotional, or they get distracted. Two things that will land you in jail. Ain't no place for feelings in this game. Fools go in, guns blazing. The wolf waits 'cause he knows a true hunt takes time." He took another drag of his cigarette and watched Carlos mull his words over, seeing if they connected with him.

Carlos rubbed the back of his faded haircut. He ran his hand down to the edge of his hair, near one of his multiple neck tattoos. After a spell, the five-foot-six Hispanic man responded.

"So that's why they say the 713 Boyz are like wolves?"

"That's right." Rico chimed in. "Slim and the three of us got that rep years ago, doin' all kinds of wild shit. We had the city shook for a while."

"We still got the city shook," The last member of their group, Terrance, who went by the nickname Trouble, interjected. Donovan waved his hand to dismiss the conversation.

"The point is, when we move, the streets notice. I'm not into picking up strays, but Rosey here said you had his back in the joint, so we'll give this a shot. Consider tonight your audition." Donovan responded, leaving Carlos slightly confused.

"Wait, who's Rosey? You mean Rico?"

"That's my nickname," Rico confirmed.

"Oh. Why do they call you that?"

"Cause he's an eternal optimist," Donovan interjected. "He's notorious for seeing everything and everyone through rose-colored glasses. In fact, had it just been him petitioning me, me and you wouldn't be having this conversation. But, like I said, Slim cosigned for you too, so we'll see what you're made of." Donovan glanced at his best friend. He knew well enough to realize he had flipped him the middle finger with his earlier insinuation.

Rico smiled and said, "This is gonna be easy. We've been plann—,"

"Don't start that 'it's gonna be easy' shit, Rosey," Trouble chimed in, shaking his head in disapproval. "Donovan, get yo boy."

"Alright, everyone, chill… Look, they're winding down over there," Donovan said.

They collectively looked across the room, then Rico looked at Trouble and Carlos.

"Okay, ladies, time to eat. You two bounce. Text us when you're set up. We'll stay here."

Carlos and Trouble nodded and headed to the front of the club. Before they got too far, Donovan pulled Trouble to the side and said, "Yo, T, let me holla at you for a sec." He looked at him with a serious face as Trouble stepped close to him, each knowing the reason for the conversation.

"Keep an eye on the new guy. He ain't one of us. One mistake, and we're all in the shit."

"I know, D. I got you. It's a full moon out tonight."

"Let's hunt."

Both men understood the code between the words. The two men exchanged a fist bump, and Trouble was on his way to the entrance of Club Indigo to leave with Rico's latest reclamation project, Carlos.

Donovan scanned the area carefully as he lit another cigarette. Clubs were never his scene, but he was enjoying the buzz of activity inside of Club Indigo. From his position he scanned the room and watched a large man in the VIP section brag for the eighth time that he was "poppin' bottles and fuckin' models tonight." He also watched as they dismissed another waitress for reasons he couldn't determine from his distance.

As *I Ain't Never Scared* by Bone Crusher blared in the background, Donovan took another puff of his cigarette. The red-hued, dimly lit club was just reaching its climax for the evening when the man they planned to rob started dancing and bringing girls into the VIP section. No matter how attractive the girls were or what songs were played, he discretely kept his focus on the six-foot-three, two-hundred-and-thirty-pound man.

Buzz… His phone sounded.

He leaned over to read his text. *Me and Los made it. 15 minutes before we're set up.* He took a drag of his cigarette and looked back towards the VIP section. His eyes were drawn to the newest waitress there serving drinks. With her light almond-colored skin, she was mesmerizing.

OH SHIT, HE THOUGHT. FROM ACROSS THE ROOM, HE NOTICED THE whiteness of her teeth and her naturally curly jet-black hair. He examined every curve and for the first time that night, got distracted.

Focus, D.

Donovan locked in and found the linebacker again, remembering that his focus for the night had to be on him. Any distraction could be a costly mistake. *One more glance can't hurt, though,* he thought to himself. Keeping his target in mind, he quickly scanned for the waitress but didn't locate her.

You were just preaching this shit, and now you're distracted by a fat ass? Back on task, D. Pay attention to the target, he ordered himself. But even with that self-imposed order, he couldn't bring himself not to take at least one more glance. He searched through the crowd for her one more time.

Buzz… An incoming text interrupted his search.

Are y'all coming? We're good to go on our end. He put his phone back in his pocket and took another puff of his cigarette.

"You know you can't smoke in here, right?"

He was stunned. The waitress he had been looking for was standing right in front of him. She was even more beautiful up close than from across the room. He took another puff of his cigarette and exhaled, then replied, "And look at me, smokin'. I've always enjoyed doing the impossible."

His response made her chuckle. "You're not a regular in here. Is it a special occasion tonight or just blowing off steam?"

"Yeah, you could call it a special occasion... We're just out here celebrating my man, Rosey."

The waitress looked towards the dance floor to see Rico dancing with a young Latin woman, then looked back at Donovan.

"Is that his real name?"

"Nah, just what we call him."

"Damn. He must be really tough."

"Now, what about that nickname makes you think he's tough?"

"Oh, come on. There's no way you make it through high school with a nickname like 'Rosey' without throwing a punch or taking a punch. And he's still pretty, so he'd have to be the one throwing the punches, or he's secretly wearing a ton of makeup."

"The trick is to find a good foundation that can cover almost anything," Donovan said with a half chuckle.

The woman laughed too and continued, "That was pretty funny. Are you also a football fan?"

"Fan? Oh, you mean the guy over there dressed like Eddie Murphy about to do a stand-up special?" The waitress chuckled a second time. He knew he wasn't as funny as she was pretending he was, but he liked how natural it felt for her to make him feel like he had a sense of humor. She replied.

"You're not into sports, are you?" she said. "That's Adrian Watson. He used to be Houston's best linebacker."

"Is that right?"

"Yeah. He signed an 80-million-dollar contract, most of it guaranteed, but got hurt. I think it's his birthday today, so he's out turning up in the town tonight. Normally he's three sheets to the wind drunk by now. I guess tonight, he's pacing himself. So, if you aren't here for him, what are you celebrating exactly? Because your friend is sure dancing his behind off right now."

Donovan glanced over at Rico, who was indeed doing too much on the dance floor. "He's just extra all the time. Kind of person you're either gonna love or hate."

"He's just... Rosey... I get it." She replied. Her question had a full answer now.

Donovan nodded and then glanced at his friend, realizing that, in fact, it was Rico's first time out since he'd come home from prison. He'd been in Huntsville Correctional Facility for the last six months on a robbery charge. So tonight, regardless of if they intended it or not, they were all celebrating and working.

Donovan and the waitress watched as the tall, lean, mixed raced man leaned into his Spanish heritage as he danced with the Latina woman who was grinding against his stonewashed black denim jeans. He looked over at his friend having a good time and nodded. Rico nodded in return, to which Donovan turned to the waitress and said,

"Babygirl, can you get my man over there a Hennessy on the rocks? That, and whatever else he's drinking tonight, is on me."

The waitress nodded. "And whose name am I putting this tab under?" she asked coyly.

"Put it under D."

"Okay. So, D as in D-e-e or the letter D?"

"Now, why does that even matter?"

"Cause I'm trying to figure out if your 'D' stands for Donald or 'D-e-e' for Demarius."

Donovan smirked and responded jokingly, "D for... get them damn drinks."

Shocked by his response, she was about to leave when he stopped her in her tracks.

"My name is Donovan," he said, still chuckling about the joke.

The waitress turned, gave him the once over, and then after a spell, responded, "Hmm... Donovan, kinda hood, kinda good... I like it."

"I'm glad you approve. And you are?"

"I'm... gonna go get those damn drinks," she replied as she winked and finished writing the order.

He enjoyed the cat-and-mouse banter that was developing between them and took another puff of his cigarette. As the woman walked past, she snatched the cigarette out of his mouth and put it out. He smiled at all five-foot-three inches of her voluptuous frame as he lit another, watching her as she walked to the main bar. He imagined what was underneath her fitted crimson crop top that exposed her well-defined midsection.

The linebacker. Shit...

He wasn't supposed to be flirting or staring at the waitress. His attention was supposed to be dedicated to watching Adrian Watson because he was working. He scanned the VIP section for the linebacker. *What the fuck?* Adrian had left the VIP section. He scanned the club for the linebacker, and his apprehension built when he couldn't locate him. *I just saw the big motherfucker,* Donovan thought to himself as he continued to scan the club. He started to wonder if the waitress was a distraction, maybe they were on to them and sent her to disarm him.

"Gotcha." He said. He located the linebacker moving towards the front of the club to leave for the night. He also noticed Rico was already making his way to the exit. *So much for Babygirl,* he thought.

Donovan scanned the room for the waitress. She held no drinks on her way back from the bar. In fact, from what he could tell, she seemed uncomfortable. The music blared as Donovan. focused his attention on the waitress. Her eyes told a story of terror. She walked away, looking repeatedly back towards the front entrance. His eyes darted to the entrance of the lounge to connect with a cinnamon-skinned man, comparable in size to him, moving through the club with the clear intent of searching for someone. He glanced back at the waitress, who he now realized knew the man because she was moving with haste towards the back of the club, close to where Donovan was watching it all unfold.

He took a puff of his cigarette and continued to observe as the woman hurried past him into the restroom, which wasn't far from the edge of the bar. Looking into her eyes as she passed, he knew she was frightened. The man was pursuing her now and dashed past him soon after, but he wasn't quite fast enough to get to her before she locked the restroom door. The man punched the door with his fist in frustration, causing a slight disturbance. Donovan watched as the man's temper boiled over.

"You better open the goddamn door before I kick this bitch in!" the man screamed angrily.

"Leave me alone, Bryan!" Her muffled yells were clear to him but were drowned out by the music in the club for the rest of the occupants.

Donovan glanced towards Rico, who was standing at the front of the club waving him to come on, signaling it was time to leave. He looked at the bathroom door again. He'd been in this situation far too many times. The jealousy of an angry lover was a familiar language from his own childhood. Donovan watched the man whose frustrations were becoming growingly unstable. As he was about to kick in the door, Donovan looked around for cameras and found none.

"Fuck this." He finished his cigarette and bolted towards the restroom. He crept up behind Bryan, pulled out his pistol, and hit him in the back of the head with brutal force, instantly rendering him unconscious. Bryan collapsed against the woman's restroom door before falling to the ground. Donovan put up his weapon and gently knocked on the door.

"You can come out, Babygirl. You ain't gotta worry about that dude anymore."

There was a pause, then shortly thereafter, the woman opened the door and walked out of the restroom. She looked down at the man lying unconscious and then back at Donovan.

"What... How?"

"Look, I don't know him or you, and I'm sure it's complicated, but... I wasn't gonna let what was about to go down happen on my watch. You feel me?"

"Um, yeah. I... Thanks. I don't know what to... Thank you," the woman responded.

Donovan extended his hand and helped her step over the sleeping man's muscular body. She took one last glance at him lying on the floor unconscious as she walked towards the bar area.

"Is he gonna..."

"He's gonna be fine. He just needed a nap, so I made him take one." Donovan knew she wanted to explain.

Her eyes shifted downward, and then she looked at him and said, "I... he... it's."

"Look, Babygirl. Like I said, I'm sure whatever it is between the two of you is complicated. I just hope you—"

"Yo, D. I ain't trying to break this up, but we gotta go now!" Rico said, cutting short his conversation.

Donovan nodded in agreement and reached into his pocket and pulled out a wad of money. He counted off five one-hundred-dollar bills and put the rest back in his pocket. He then folded the bills and put them in the woman's hand.

"Take this. Consider it a tip for great service tonight. Should be enough to get a place for the night if you guys live together. Or, even if you don't, stay someplace else until you figure it out. I gotta go. It was nice to meet you." He could tell she received his words with the sincerity he meant them with.

"Thank you... I don't know what to s—"

"Yo, D! Right now," Rico repeated, to which Donovan agreed.

"Take care, Babygirl."

2
THE WOLVES

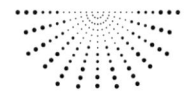

"Will you slow the fuck down? Any closer, we're going to be in the back seat of that motherfucker," Rico said as they trailed the black SUV in front of them.

"Relax, I know what I'm doing," Donovan replied. Rico nodded and then rolled his eyes before he said, "We wouldn't be in this situation if you weren't trying to bang the waitress."

"That's why I got you watching my back."

"Don't make a habit of it, hermano. It looks like it's just him and the driver tonight," Rico said as he loaded the clip into his .45 caliber Smith & Wesson. Donovan looked on as Rico continued his thoughts.

"Ten people leave the club, and none of them are rolling with him? The dude is really trying to hold on to his image."

"You know athletes, they can't let it go. He'll spend his fortune trying to relive those days. The thing is, once nobody cares... nobody cares," Donovan responded.

Rico put the gun in the waistband of his pants and took a shot of the Tanqueray gin kept in the back seat. He handed Donovan the bottle who also took a sip and handed it back before saying,

"I have it on good authority from Adrian Watson's former dealer that he's done using. In fact, all he takes now is a glass of Hennessy X.O. with a combination of crushed Viagra and Ambien pills."

"So, what's the plan? Wait until he's good and drunk and passed out?"

"Something like that."

"Hold on, did you just say Viagra?" Rico asked inquisitively. Donovan nodded in response and continued,

"So, turns out, his driver is also his lover. On nights like tonight, he lets the guy suck him to sleep. Then, on the way out the door, the driver turns up the music and cuts on a few lights to let everyone know Adrian is still a bad boy. Meanwhile, he's fast asleep in his soundproof bedroom."

"Wait, no judgment, but are you telling me that the Texans' most eligible linebacker, baby daddy to that fine ass super model Takari Watson, is really a wide receiver?" Rico asked.

"The point is when he goes to sleep, we have about a good hour window before the first patrol comes through this neighborhood. What about your friend? Will she be able to take care of the guard?"

"Oh, don't worry about the patrol. Melinda's supposed to meet him as we speak, and she looks mighty fuckable. This is their first night together, and he's bringing tulips."

"Well, that's special."

"I'm sure once he gets over there, she'll slip him something, and the only thing he's gonna be patrolling 'till sunrise is the back of his eyelids. And get this, she gave us a discount because of that thing we handled for her last month," Rico said as he put on his black gloves, getting ready for action.

"Well then, we're good, as long as we can trust your boy Carlos to not do anything stupid."

"There you go with that shit again. D, I told you he had my back when I was in the joint. Besides, we gotta take the training wheels off at some point, eh?"

Donovan ignored the statement. The plan was solid, but Carlos was the area that concerned him the most. "All I'm saying is that's the kind of cat that can fuck up an easy score like this," he said.

"You worry too much, amigo. Los doesn't want to go back to jail, and neither do I."

"Good, because we will get jammed up if we panic."

"Aye, mamacita, chill already. This is a fool-proof plan. Besides, we know what they'd do on the inside to a pretty chica like you," Rico said jokingly, gesturing over to his comrade with a kiss face.

"Fool-proof plans only prove fools exist, and you make that face again, I'm gonna shoot you in your kneecap."

"Bitch, you can't aim."

"Man, hand me the goddamn bottle and see if Trouble and Carlos are still good to go."

Rico relented and handed Donovan the liquor. He then sent a text to their companions, and within an instant, he got a reply.

"He said it's a full moon out tonight."

Donovan understood the code. The 713 Boyz, his crew, were on schedule.

Donovan handed Rico the bottle of gin they were both nursing as they turned from the main road into a winding neighborhood known as Shadow Creek Ranch. It was a suburb on the outskirts of Houston and one of the primary residential neighborhoods of the upper middle class and filthy rich. Adrian Watson had a home so big that his was one of only four houses on his street. From what Donovan could tell, the other homes weren't occupied often. He assumed they were homes for other athletes to live in during the off-season. Smith Security paid a guard to patrol all the homes in this part of the neighborhood, but that guard was currently preoccupied thanks to Rico's friend, Melinda.

"Quick and easy," he said to himself, buying into some of Rico's optimism. They believed the athlete kept over 100 grand in cash in his home's safe, and opening safes and locks was Rico's specialty.

As they pulled into the neighborhood, they parked three streets away and sat in silence until they got the text from Trouble, who used codes to communicate in case anyone ever confiscated their phones, or they lost one. His latest text was simple.

It's a full moon out tonight.

The code was clear; it was go time. They watched as the driver's car passed them on its way out of the neighborhood.

"T said we're good," Donovan said.

"Then it's time to hunt or be hunted," Rico said, as Donovan checked his pistol.

"Tell everyone to set their timer. We got forty-five minutes in and out."

Donovan and Rico both set their watches for forty-five minutes. Donovan drove over to the Watson home with his lights off. When the pair arrived, the high beam of a car's flashing lights greeted them. It was the signal from Trouble that everything was all clear. Both cars pulled into the driveway, and the quartet exited their vehicles.

As they converged on the door, Donovan said, "You all know the layout of the house. We got one hour. When our forty-five-minute timer goes off, it's time to wrap it up. Once Rico gets this door open, I'm going to cut the alarm and disable the security feed. Rico will work on the safe. You two get to that bedroom and tie up Adrian Watson."

"How much is the split?" Carlos interjected.

Donovan looked at him blankly before responding, "Who gives a shit? We're here now. Like I was say—"

"Hold on, we're all risking our lives here. We should know for how much."

"You don't have to risk shit, Los. You're free to wait in the car."

"We don't have time for this right now," Rico interjected. "Look, Carlos. We have no idea how much cash is in the house, but they say he keeps 100 large on him at all times. We're not taking heirlooms. That's the shit that brings out emotion and ultimately gets your ass locked up. There should be more than enough cash around here tonight, alright? Now, if you're done squabbling, we have a job to do. The wolves are out. Let's eat." The men all pulled down their masks. Each of them displaying the face of a different wolf. Rico tapped

Donovan on the shoulder as he glared at Carlos before heading to the door.

Rico broke in and he and Donovan entered first. They went directly to the trophy room, a shrine to Adrian Watson's accomplishments, where they had it on good authority he kept his primary safe and security footage. The amount of detail Rico could find out about a home always impressed Donovan. Years of working with his dad in construction gave him a knack for getting scarce information. This score was already better than expected. Everything was top of the line and done deliberately to provoke awe. Looking at the bronzed, life-sized mural of Adrian Watson in the middle of the sports room, he realized this score would be hard to fight temptation. He looked at the floor designs to locate the safe.

"There is a video hard drive in the cabinet behind the safe."

The pair moved toward their assignments. Donovan worked on the security footage while Rico worked on the safe.

After a spell, Donovan announced, "I wiped the footage, and I got the hard dive. We should be good on my end." He stood up in his black jumpsuit and turned on his newest toy, a voice modulator he had customized for his mask.

"How's it coming?"

"The safe is coming along fine, Darth Negro. What? You 'bout to go fight Luke Skywalker with that shit on?"

"I'm just testing it out. How much longer do you think?" Donovan asked.

"I think... I'm just about..."

Click. The heavy metal door of the safe sprung open.

"Bingo."

Donovan watched as Rico opened the safe. The two pulled the cash from the safe and put it in a black bag. Rico was disappointed that there wasn't as much cash as they thought.

"Thirty-seven thousand?" he said in frustration.

"Almost 10 apiece. Not the best haul, but maybe there's more cash in the bedroom."

Rico tossed 5 thousand to Donovan, who put it in his back pocket.

"Finders' fee for us, so we only found thirty-two."

Donovan laughed. "That's what I counted. Let's get out of here befo—"

"Hold on, did you hear that?"

"Hear what?"

"I don't know. It sounded like glass breaking or something," Rico said as he reached for his pistol.

Donovan listened intently, but it was hard to hear anything other than the drowning baseline of 50 Cents' *I Got Money* blasting through the house.

"Dog, it's probably part of the music or something."

Pop! Pop! Pop!

The sounds were unmistakable. The pair ducked and made eye contact confirming they were both aware they'd heard gunshots.

"Yeah, definitely not the music," Rico stated.

Donovan took out his pistol.

"Find a way to turn this damn music off, then meet me upstairs," he barked at his friend as he headed for the stairs, moving with a sense of urgency. He wasn't sure what was happening, but it didn't matter, he was ready for anything. As he got to the door of the master bedroom, he glanced briefly at his pistol to make sure there was one in the chamber should he need to use it. He took a breath and slowly opened the door with his pistol up, looking to end any immediate danger in his presence. As he entered, his eyes scoured the room as the music got louder. Adrenaline surged through his body as he turned the corner. Suddenly, the music went out.

Fuck this.

He darted around the corner of the hallway, and his eyes widened.

"What in the hell?!"

3
MY MIND'S PLAYING TRICKS ON ME

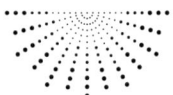

"What did y'all do?" Donovan asked as he took off his wolf mask and looked at the football player lying on the floor, bleeding profusely from his abdomen. He followed the trail of blood. There were footprints and smears of blood on the bed comforter. Broken glass covered the ground. He turned and looked at Carlos, who was holding the gun, shaking and nervous.

His eyes widened, "You shot him?"

"He was coming for me, and I—"

"Trouble, what the fuck happened?" Donovan barked, ignoring the would-be excuse from Carlos.

Trouble began to explain. "It went like you said it would, D. He was lying down, and we tied his big ass up to the chair. Tied him up good too. I saw there was an extra safe, and, well, you know, I'm thinking, 'Man, let's get some of the cash that might be in there.' Thing was, the safe was already open because that's where ole buddy keeps his championship rings. So, you know our code, leave the personal shit, take the cash, cause them heirlooms 'n shit will have your ass in jail for a while. And I'm tryin' to tell the new guy about this, but he's like fuck it, and grabs ole buddy's championship college ring. That's when the football player loses it. He's beggin' and says, 'Take anything, but not that one.' Los walks over to him and said some shit like, 'I'm gonna take in seconds what it took you a lifetime to earn.' That's when I heard the chair break. This big motherfucker busted it up on some incredible hulk shit and started whooping Carlos' ass. Well, you know I have no problem handling things with my hands, so I come over and hit him with a two-piece combo, extra spicy. That right hook was about to have his ass back in the chair when this one turned into Mel Gibson, on some Lethal weapon shit." Donovan rubbed his eyes, using his thumb and index finger to calm his frustration. After a spell he turned and asked. "Why did you do it, Carlos?"

"What the fuck, D? I thought you said not to use real names," Carlos fired back. Donovan looked at the football player. He was still alive, but bleeding heavily. "Man, what the fuck you think we're gonna have to do with this dude? Take him to the hospital? You gotta finish what you started."

As he looked down at the football player, he could tell he was fighting for his life and losing the battle. If he could yell, he would. If he could get up, he'd do that too, but all he could do was bleed. Donovan heard footsteps behind him as Rico approached.

"Holy shit," Rico said, processing the scene.

Donovan cut his eyes back to his best friend. "Yeah, thank your boy Carlos Stallone over there."

Rico looked over at Carlos and said, "You shot the motherfucker?"

"I didn't have a choice."

"Nah, you had a choice, and you chose wrong," Trouble interjected, "Man, we should've waited on Slim to get out of jail to do this one, D. I swear I'm not going down for a hom—"

"That's enough! We'll talk about that shit off the field. Right now, we got bigger problems than Carlos' heart pumping pink Kool-aid."

Carlos waved Donovan off dismissively as Donovan began to assess the scene. He assumed that because of their scuffle DNA was everywhere.

"What's the plan?" Trouble asked.

Donovan and Rico both looked at the football player who was breathing heavily, clinging to life. The two men glanced over at Trouble and Carlos, who were both feeling inadequate. As upset as he was, he knew this wasn't the time for the needed discussion. The soundproof room had muffled the first gunshot. He had barely heard it while inside the house and knew it wouldn't be the last shot fired in this home. Donovan folded his arms and examined the room. He looked at the blood on the floor seeping into the carpet, which would soak into the wood and stain the concrete. He looked at his watch.

"We're 20 minutes into this and running out of time. Carlos, at least tell me you know where the shell casings are," Donovan said, hoping their luck would improve.

He looked at Carlos and knew there was no reprieve. The silence was deafening against the ice gray soundproof walls. It continued to grow until, finally, Rico broke the silence and the growing tension.

"So, what you thinking, D? Want to pull a running man?" Rico asked, also assessing the situation.

"It would fall apart too easily. He's too famous."

"What about a wipe me down?"

"Too much DNA, and we don't know where the shell casings ended up. Besides, now we're up against the clock. There's not enough time for that."

"Our only option is to..."

"Disco Inferno," the pair said in unison.

Trouble nodded in agreement, but Carlos, unfamiliar with their internal slang, stood confused.

Donovan didn't care, he didn't have time to. The clock was ticking and every second at a crime scene was one second too long. He scanned the room differently now that he knew what needed to be done.

Carlos, still confused, confronted Rico who was making his way back to the main hallway.

"Something on your mind, Carlos?" Rico asked.

"Yeah... Running man? Wipe me down? Disco.... whatever. Exactly what the hell are you guys talking about?"

Rico explained their code to Carlos as Donovan continued looking for a solution to their current dilemma.

"This motherfucker has to disappear, right? So, if we pull a running man, we make it look like he abruptly left town and leave enough misdirection to leave the cops wondering. A wipe me down is us leaving the body here, but wiping down our prints and—"

"Why are we doing any of that?" Carlos interjected. "We should just get out of here. We got the video footage and the cash. Let's go."

The words angered Donovan, who barged into the conversation.

"That's exactly what you'd like to do, isn't it? Just leave a mess like this and run. You just shot one of the richest and most famous men in the whole damn city, and your solution is to run and leave all this fucking evidence? Blood, broken glass, DNA, oh, and the fucking shell casings for a gun I'm sure you've probably used before tonight. Not to mention, if he survives, an eyewitness. How long do you think it would take for them to pick our asses up?"

"He will not remember this night! He's fucking drunk and high."

"You stupid motherf—" Donovan interrupted, he rubbed his forehead in frustration. He pointed at the athlete, who was bleeding heavily and continued. "You got knots all over your head and are gonna have two black eyes... Do you honestly think... Get your boy, Rico. I don't have time for this shit."

Rico stood between Donovan and Carlos, motioning his hands to signal Donovan to calm down. Rico turned to Carlos.

"He got shot, Los, and adrenaline is pumping hard into his system. He's remembering everything now. The only way we can make sure he doesn't talk, is to make sure he can't talk."

"Wait, what?" Carlos asked, still confused.

Infuriated, Donovan threw his hands up in frustration and pushed Rico to the side and said.

"That's right, you stupid son of a bitch. He's one of the most famous athletes in the entire city. You'd been better off shooting the mayor. The moment you shot him, you made us all accessories to a homicide. You gotta finish what you started."

He examined Carlos, whose eyes betrayed him.

Donovan saw his fear and hesitation. He looked at the football player still clinging to life. He decided something needed to go right tonight.

"Give me this," he said, snatching Carlos' 9-millimeter pistol. He grabbed two pillows off of the bed and made his way over to Adrian Watson, who was struggling to speak. He was fighting to make out words.

"Please, man, just take... the money. Take everything... Please... Don't do this," the athlete begged.

Donovan leaned in and looked the man in his eyes. He could see the man's fear as tears rolled from his eyes. Donovan shook his head. He was on top of the world an hour ago, but now he was dying.

"You were a hell of an athlete, homeboy. Sorry it ends like this."

"Please, man. I'm begging you. I won't say nothing. Just let me live... I got kids."

Donovan knelt down and looked the dying man in his eyes. Even if he wanted to save him, the odds of him making it to the hospital alive were dwindling rapidly.

"You don't have much time left. I think it's best you make peace with the Most High, partna."

He watched as waves of fear and anger settled into peace and acceptance in the banks of Adrian's mind. He was as ready as he would ever be.

"Close your eyes and count backward. This won't hurt none. Rest easy." Donovan placed the pillows over Adrian's face as he tried to resist with what little strength he had left in his failing body.

Pop!

The bullet entered Adrian Watson's head, ending his misery with the stillness only death can bring. The four men stood in silence for a moment as the plan went south. Donovan looked at Rico.

"Fool-proof plan, huh?"

"You want to talk about this now or in prison?" Rico responded.

Conceding the point, Donovan turned and gave the gun to Trouble. "OK, here's the plan, T. Take this on your next fishing trip. Rico, turn the music back up and meet me in the kitchen. Carlos, you and

Trouble wrap this big motherfucker's body up and put it in the trunk... our trunk. We can't have any more mistakes."

Donovan moved into the hallway with Rico. The sands of time were shifting against them. They were past schedule which put them in an uncharted territory for the night. As they headed down the stairs, Rico said aloud.

"I saw some gasoline tanks when we were on the way in. Let's hope they have some fuel in them."

The quartet headed downstairs to their assignments. Rico joined Donovan in the kitchen, while Trouble opened the garage and moved their getaway vehicles into position, parking one in the empty garage bay. He then went to his car for the large black plastic bags he kept for unforeseen circumstances. Killing one of the most famous athletes in the city on a simple smash and grab definitely qualified as an unforeseen circumstance.

Trouble walked in shaking his head while holding up a canister. "We got one gas can, and it's half full."

Donovan looked at Rico, who shook his head dismissing the unasked question. Finally, he said, "It ain't enough D." Donovan agreed and then turned to Trouble.

"You gotta make it work, T. Use that shit and make a trail up the stairs into that bedroom. Use the liquor bottles in the game room for whatever you can't cover with the gas. There's enough of that shit to burn this entire block down."

Donovan began raiding the pantries in search of flammable liquids when Rico chimed in, "Yo, D, check it out."

He walked over to join him and saw the large vats of vegetable oil sitting on the floor. He pumped his fist in the air, "Finally, some good fuckin' news."

He took one of the large vats and put it on the counter while Rico searched for the largest pots he could find and turned the stove burners on high.

Carlos walked in, confused by what he was seeing, and asked, "What are you doing? You seriously can't be trying to have a cookout right now."

"Nah, goof ass, they gonna start a fire," Trouble said in response.

Rico looked up, and finally, his frustration matched Donovan's. "Look, if we don't move our asses, we're gonna have all the time in the world to explain this shit to you in lockup. Get the body in the goddamn trunk so we can do what we need to do!"

Trouble and Carlos went to secure the body while Donovan and Rico poured vegetable oil into areas of the house that would ultimately lead to the fire consuming the house.

After twenty minutes, the body was in the trunk, and the oil was where it needed to be.

"Ok, D. We poured the liquor through the bedroom, and the body is in your car, so we're good."

"Alright, we gotta get out of here," he replied. The oil had come to its boiling point. Donovan ushered everyone outside to the back driveway. He then found pot handlers, and he and his best friend poured the oil on the kitchen floor and in other critical areas to help ignite the flame. As they walked outside, he turned on the faucet. He walked over to Trouble, who was keeping a lookout.

"T, we're gonna get on the road and get this body out of here. In exactly five minutes, if this fire hasn't started, light this rag and supercharge that bitch. I'm pretty sure that water hitting that hot oil is gonna cause a grease fire, but no matter what, make sure that fire starts before you go anywhere. We better hope we put enough of this around that the alcohol catches on fire and takes out the top floor."

"We're going the back road towards the club, you all head in the opposite direction. Go to the original spot and don't move 'till we get there."

Donovan looked at Trouble to reiterate his need to watch the new guy. Then, he got in the car, with Rico in the passenger seat, and started the engine. He rolled down the window with last words for his friend Trouble.

"Five minutes. No phone calls, not even on the burner in case we get pinched."

"You bet," Trouble said as he nodded in agreement while the pair took off their black jumpsuits, stuffed them in a bag, and pulled out of the garage in the black sedan. They kept the lights off until they were out of the cul-de-sack and onto the main road heading towards Club Indigo.

Donovan lit a cigarette as he drove. After a spell, he exhaled and said, "A pro athlete, man? How stupid is that motherfucker!?"

"I know... I know, D. It was sloppy."

"We never had these problems with Slim. Trouble's right. We should've waited."

"Shit, you're telling me? I gotta rearrange my whole goddamn fantasy football roster behind this amateur hour shit."

"Rico."

"My bad, homes. I thought he was ready. I was wrong... But the split is 3 ways now since we just gave the motherfucker a get out of jail free card."

"This shit ain't worth it, not at 10 times the price... And that motherfucker was coked up too?"

"He was definitely tweaking. Having him involved was on me."

"Not on you alone, Slim too. I know we couldn't have waited on him. No telling when he's getting out, but... We're breaking our own rules, man. We need to keep the circle tight until Slim gets home. I mean, we gotta take this fucking body because honestly, I don't trust that motherfucker to get it done right and we didn't shoot anybody, but he looks like a snitch to me."

"You gonna bitch about this until we get this corpse in the ground? Cause if so, I'll work on that fantasy team while we're on the way to dig the hole."

"I might. Hell, don't make it seem like I didn't try to warn you that he was bad ne—"

"Bad news. Ay, Dios mío! Let's just go kill him too and put him in the plot next to the stiff in the trunk, so I don't have to hear about this crap for the rest of my life."

There was a brief silence, but after a moment, Donovan spoke.

"Look. All I'm saying is the less he knows, the better. Only me and you know where the body is going, and T is going to get rid of the whistle we used on his next fishing trip. We just don't need no more loose en—"

"Holy Shit!"

"This better not be about your fantasy football team cause I—"

"Nah... shit... Shit, shit, shit!"

"What is it?" Donovan asked, wondering what had startled his friend.

"There's a cop behind us."

4
CROOKED OFFICER

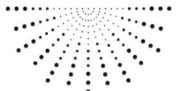

Donovan glanced in the rear-view mirror. The cruiser's lights were off, but he was definitely gaining speed. He'd dealt with law enforcement enough to know when he was being followed. This was no exception.

"Fuck! How long was he behind us?" He asked, trying to figure out what to do next. Rico took a sip of the gin and handed the bottle to his friend.

"I don't know."

"You think he clocked us back in the neighborhood?"

"I don't think so, but I'm not sure." Donovan handed his friend the liquor bottle to stash and watched the cruiser in the rear-view mirror. He could tell the cop was picking up speed and would be right on top of them shortly. He glanced at Rico, who was looking in the side-view mirror, arriving at the same conclusion. They needed to get off the road. Rico turned to Donovan and asked.

"We good on the car?"

"The plates are clean, but let's not press our luck. You know what we got in the trunk." He glanced again, and the officer was definitely gaining speed. His instincts told him this officer was going to pull them over. Rico rubbed his hands across his face.

"Ay, Dios mío. Pull over there at that Waffle House. He can't have probable cause if we're off the road, in a restaurant full of people," Rico said abruptly.

Donovan nodded and made a sharp turn, darting quickly into an empty parking space. He parked the car and turned to Rico, who was about to take his gun inside when Donovan stopped him.

"If it comes down to it, I'll deal with the cop. You get rid of the body."

The two nodded at each other. It wasn't long before he could see the police officer waiting in traffic to turn into the Waffle House in his peripheral vision.

"Fuck, man, I told you!" Rico said nervously.

"Play it cool, man. Let's just keep it moving."

Donovan walked into the restaurant and scanned the area as they walked past the server. His eyes lit up when he came across the third booth from the restroom near the back of the restaurant.

"I'll be damned," he said, surprised by who he saw. The waitress he'd left abruptly at the club was sitting at the table with a friend who was clearly drunk. Donovan walked over to the woman, and sat in the opposite stall, startling her. Rico sat directly across from her friend in the booth as Donovan said,

"Look, Babygirl, I'm sorry about coming in so abruptly. I hate to do this to you now, but there's a good chance a cop is about to walk into this building and start fucking with us."

"And what? You trying to get me locked up too? Boy, bye."

"It ain't like that. We ain't done nothing to nobody. I swear. It's just late and... Well, we fit the description for anything going on in this city."

"That's unless you're on a date."

Her quick thinking matched his own, even more so, she didn't seem scared. Something that her friend, who was clearly a sloppy drunk, didn't seem to have an issue with either. Donovan watched her eyes as they darted towards the front door and as expected, a police officer walked into the restaurant, scanning for someone. Donovan looked over at the woman in front of him, who, on cue, laughed hysterically.

After her outburst, she exclaimed, "And this drunk bitch here! Now, what were y'all thinking? You know Amanda can't hold no damn liquor."

Donovan glanced at Rico, who laughed and went along with it.

"Man, you know what? I didn't know she was that much of a lightweight."

"Rico, please, now you know damn good and well Amanda has always been a lightweight. Remember that pool party last year? Two drinks, and the heffa almost drowned," she replied.

Donovan calmed himself as he watched the woman he had just met provide an alibi for anyone within earshot. It impressed him that she remembered Rico's name from earlier in the night. He got in on the action.

"Yeah, she ain't never been able to hold her liquor."

Almost on cue, Amanda sat up. "Oh, fuck you all, I can hold my liq..." She held her mouth, got up and ran to the restroom. She was right inside the restroom door when Donovan heard the splatter of a night's worth of liquor hit the floor.

"Cleanup on aisle three," Rico said as the three of them laughed.

It was exactly what they needed, still Donovan could feel the gaze of the officer on them. He glanced out the side of his eye and observed the officer asking the server something in the general area about their table. All he could think about was the body in the trunk of the stolen car. He knew the plates were clean, but if he had to open the trunk, not only would they be going to jail, they'd be on death row. He couldn't take the chance. He needed to act, and fast.

His new acquaintance grabbed his hand as he reached for his pistol. "Baby, you're gonna have to help me get her in the car, you know that right?"

He felt the woman's grip provide a soothing feeling to his tension. He made eye contact with her. She also knew he was about to make a decision that he couldn't come back from.

"You got me baby?" she asked. Her question implying more than its surface meaning.

He relaxed and nodded his head in agreement. "Yeah... I got you Babygirl."

It was right then he heard the voice he was trying to avoid.

"Excuse me, folks." The officer, a five-foot eight white male with a buzz cut, interjected. "Ma'am, do you know these men?"

Babygirl cut her eyes to the officer. "Well, let's see, I'm holding this one's hand, and we're about to order food, so I'm going to say that's a yes."

The officer smirked and nodded his head in agreement with a hint of sarcasm.

"It's just that normally if a woman is out with other women and one of them is drunk, she goes with her to the restroom to check on her... and yet here you are."

"A. You don't know her or me. B. If I had to follow that chick to the restroom every time she got drunk, I'd be a goddamn janitor. C. I've had a long day at work, so my feet are tired, and D. I don't know what that has to do with why you're at our table asking us uninvited questions. The police officer turned his head to the door, then looked back at Babygirl.

"Where are you all coming from?"

"Club Indigo."

"And these men were with you all night?"

Still holding Donovan's hand, she lifted them both in the air. "If you look at the stamp on both of our hands, it shows we were both at Club Indigo."

"So where –"

"I no longer care to discuss the details of my evening, officer," she fired back. The officer turned his attention to Donovan, who locked eyes with him.

"OK... let's try this another way. Sir, if you were at Club Indigo, why were you driving from the opposite direction previously?"

Donovan was about to respond when the woman he'd been calling

Babygirl for the last few hours pulled out her phone and started to record the interaction.

"Oh, go ahead, baby, I'm just live streaming how Officer... Cunningham, I think that's what that badge says, is about to make a poor life choice by sitting here harassing two United States military combat veterans while we're trying to have a simple ending to our night. All because his job gives him the authority to act on his feelings about how he doesn't like black and brown men."

"Ma'am, put your phone down. I don't have any problem with veterans or Hispanics."

"So that's an admission you don't like black men? Convenient how you left them out. Do tell, Officer Cunningham. How long have you been profiling minorities, specifically black men, in your career?" she responded as loud as she could, gathering the attention of the other patrons in the restaurant.

The officer glanced around at a growing audience who was starting to pay attention. "Ma'am, I'm not gonna say it again. Put down your ph—"

"You can say it 'till you're red, white, and blue in the face. It is my first amendment right to record my interactions with an officer of the law."

"Not if you're being disruptive."

"You have got to be kidding. Now everybody was just fine before you got here harassing these two combat veterans trying to have a good night out after defending our country for the last 18 months. And on the first night they don't have to worry about life or death, here you come. If you ask me, or anyone in here, the only disruptive force that me and all these other witnesses see, is you. Now we've answered your questions within reason and no longer wish to, so unless you just feel like this is the night you want to throw away your entire career inside this Waffle House; I think it's best you go find some other minorities to profile."

The officer looked around as other patrons began to pull out their phones. His tone changed as he looked at Donovan.

"It wasn't... I'm not... Sorry for bothering you... the both of you.

Thank you for your service. Make sure your friend gets home safely," he said as he pointed to Amanda, who was walking back to the booth.

A wave of relief washed over Donovan as the officer left. In disbelief, he looked at Babygirl, startled by what had just taken place as her food arrived and she proceeded to eat her hash browns as if nothing had happened. He'd had run-ins with the police before. It never ended well. He still wasn't sure how this one ended the way it did. He looked at Rico, who was just as stunned, and back to Babygirl, who was now cutting her pancakes.

"Pass me the syrup, if you don't mind," she said nonchalantly.

Donovan glanced at Rico, who was also still processing what had just happened, and chuckled, which built into laughter.

After a spell, he asked, "Yo! What the fuck was that? Like, how did you do that just now?"

"Oh, please. As soon as I saw that buzz cut, I knew that cop was not here to protect or serve. Whatever you did, or didn't do, I know you didn't need to be going anywhere with him. Besides, I kinda owe you," she said as she took a bite of her pancake.

Still in disbelief, Donovan sat quietly. He glanced at Rico, who was just beginning his own line of questioning. After some internal deliberation, Rico finally asked the question he'd been thinking about.

"OK, I'm with you on that and all, but how did you know I was a vet?"

"Well, I saw the tattoo on your forearm. That's the Navy crest. I thought about joining before I went to college, so I knew what it looked like. I also know that cops, on average, seem to have respect for military men. The rest was marketing, and since I'm going to be the best in the world when it comes to that profession, it was easy target practice... no pun intended."

"Very clever," Donovan finally said as he rejoined the conversation.

"You're either feeling pressure, or you're applying it growing up in the Tre. We're used to cops like that. Sometimes you just gotta punch a bully in the mouth," she said before she ate the rest of her meal.

He was in awe of her confidence. The same beautiful waitress he'd met earlier, who'd hid in the bathroom from her assailant, was now a fierce lioness. He wanted to know more about her.

"You're from third ward?" He asked as she smiled, nodded, and replied.

"Born and raised. What about you two?"

"South Park. Not too far fro—"

"Yo, D. Hate to cut this short, but we gotta go do that thing, remember?" Rico said, interrupting the conversation and bringing things back into focus.

Donovan realized it was well past time to go.

"Yeah, I think we all need to leave before constable Klansman comes back with reinforcements. I'll have them box up my food. If you can do me one more favor and help me with this one to the car?" she said as she winked at Donovan.

He laughed and nodded. The night had taken him to the brink of disaster, and while his night was far from finished, at that moment, he felt the bliss only a beautiful woman could bring to a man's life. Thinking about her in that way made him realize that throughout this entire ordeal, he didn't know the one thing he should know about the waitress who had just saved him from a life sentence. As the quartet left, Donovan asked what he'd been dying to know since he first laid eyes on her.

"So are you going to tell me your na—"

"That asshole is still here. He's waiting across the street," she said, cutting him off.

The hair on the back of his neck raised as her words hit him with a sobering dose of reality. He wasn't out of the woods yet. Donovan glanced out of the corner of his eye slightly toward a nestled area directly across the street from the Waffle House. The cop had left the parking lot, but he didn't go far. Donovan knew he was waiting for them.

Shit, he thought to himself. This was trouble, which would only get worse if they didn't figure out something quickly.

"Rosey, make sure you don't step on any roaches because I saw a few across the street."

Rico picked up on the code without breaking stride. "You sure? I thought they scattered earlier."

"Nah, I don't think they ever left. Just waiting."

Rico wiped his brow. Donovan knew this friend wanted to run. He did too. While he wasn't sure why the cop was so determined to harass them, he knew if they got in that car, they'd be going to jail. He wondered if Carlos and Trouble were already caught, and the cop was just waiting to open the trunk to tie it all together.

How else could he know? Maybe he's waiting for a search warrant, he thought as his mind continued to race.

Babygirl interrupted his train of thought , "He's fishing cause if he had anything on either of you, that stunt I pulled inside wouldn't have worked."

"So, uh... What do you suggest we do?"

"Well, for starters, act like we're on a date. Put your arm around me. Marketing, remember?"

"That's right… marketing."

"Next, you can help me get Amanda in the car, and maybe we can talk in the parking lot for a while. Wait this asshole out."

"I can't ask you to do that for us," he said.

Without acknowledging him, she looked over at Rico. "Are you sure he's from South Park? He's acting like a north-sider."

Donovan and Rico both laughed at the statement.

"See, now you look like you're on a date… un-bothered. You see what I'm talkin' 'bout? Now hold my hand," she said casually.

He didn't push back and just went with it. She was smart, witty, and could handle herself on the fly. She was a soldier who knew when it was time to ride.

As the quartet arrived at Amanda's car, Rico put Amanda, who was sobering up and started making conversation with him, in the car. Donovan's attention was on Babygirl. As soon as Amanda was in the car, Babygirl wrapped her arms around his broad, muscular shoulders.

"What's this?"

"I mean, we're dating according to that, what did you call him? Roach?"

"You caught that, huh?" he said with a slight chuckle.

"I did. So again, it's all about the optics. I'm thinking that maybe if we make out for a bit, he'll realize ain't nobody worried about his ass, and he'll go find someone else to fuck with. What do you say?"

He looked at her full lips and couldn't deny her logic.

"Sounds like the best plan I've heard all night."

He leaned in to kiss her, and she embraced him. It was natural. Their lips met, and their tongues knew exactly where the other one was at all times as their dance of emotions was cemented by this action.

As they kissed, Donovan heard a rumbling and felt a flash of heat. A wave of heat caught them both off guard.

Boom!

The pair unlocked their lips from one another and glanced at the officer as he turned on his lights and pulled out onto the main road. "Whirp!" his siren screamed as his engine revved to its maximum. He darted past them towards the direction of Adrian Watson's home.

Babygirl asked what everyone was wondering, "Was that an explosion?"

"Uh... yeah, I think it was?" Donovan said, slightly confused, although he knew where it had to come from. The fire he set had to have worked better than expected.

"Hermano! We gotta roll. Like right, right now!" Rico said animatedly.

Donovan knew his friend was pissed when he spoke Spanish. Releasing the woman from his grip and fighting his nature to hold her, he forced himself to accept reality. He looked at her lips, wishing he had more time to explore their fullness, but he knew he couldn't. There was a long night ahead of him, and he had just caught his first break. He looked at her sparkling brown eyes, the only thing that drew more heat than the explosion they'd all just felt. His tone filled with remorse as he turned to the waitress and said, "Yeah, Babygirl, Rico's right. We gotta head out."

"Alright, well, it was nice meeting you... Donovan."

As he started to walk off, he thought about his chance encounter with this woman who had needed his help and, in turn, had saved him. He thought about their kiss. Her sweet tender lips feeling as natural to him as his own skin. He wished he could have another. Although the window of opportunity to make an escape had just opened, his window to get to know her better was closing rapidly. He stopped and turned around.

"Yo... So... You're not gonna give me your name, your number, nothing?"

Babygirl smiled. She walked towards him and kissed him again, this time more passionately. He could feel her breasts pressed against his chest as she leaned into him with a sense of familiarity. As he became erect, she pulled away and said,

"I'll give it to you... tomorrow at 4 o'clock. Go to the place they serve the king's special."

"Hold up. You want me to meet you where?" he asked, confused by the statement.

She smirked. "You have all the clues you need if you're really from the south side of Houston. Besides, you've found me twice. The third times the charm, right? Four p.m., don't be late," she said as she kissed him on the cheek and got into her car.

He watched as she drove off before turning to his friend, who was already pulling their car up. As he got in the passenger seat, he could feel the frustration of his best friend. The two drove in silence, constantly checking to see if they were being followed. It was twenty minutes before either of them said anything.

"What a fucking night," Donovan said, finally breaking the silence.

"This is why we the wolves, baby!" Rico said in a burst of laughter resulting in both men making the howling imitation of a wolf. While relieved about their favorable odds, they both understood the gravity that the night was just beginning. A man still had to be buried.

5
TELL ME SOMETHING GOOD

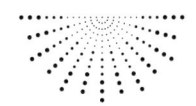

"And while several estates in the area were destroyed, none of the residents were at home except former Texans, all-pro linebacker Adrian Watson. It remains inconclusive if the athlete was at his estate, but family and friends haven't heard from him.

When we asked Chief Peterson of the Brazoria County fire district if he had any more information about last night's explosion, here's what he had to say:

'The fire originated at the home of Adrian Watson but was near an undetected rupture in the gas pipeline. When the flame activated it, there was a massive explosion. While we're doing all we can to determine if Mr. Watson was a casualty, the sheer volume of heat from the explosion would make it highly unlikely for us to find any human remains.'

That was Chief Peterson on the update of the explosion in southwest Houston last night and the status of the Texans' own Adrian Watson. We tried to talk to his driver, the last person to see him alive, but he was understandably distr—"

Click.

Donovan turned off the radio as he and Rico sat in front of their next target's home.

"So, we spent all last night burying that body for nothing?" Rico said half-jokingly, to which Donovan laughed hard at his friend's morbid sense of humor.

"Hell, my arms still hurt from digging that hole but I'm not gonna lie, that was the luckiest thing that has happened to me. Ever."

Donovan lit a cigarette as the pair watched the house in front of them.

Rico continued, "Man, if I knew we would've gotten away clean like that, I would've taken those rings Carlos got his ass whooped for."

"We ain't clean yet. That cop had a hard-on for us last night."

"Nah, he was just being a dick. Besides, even if he did, what in the hell is he gonna say? We were literally in front of him when the motherfucker exploded. Besides, your girl handled him well. Telling that cop we were with her all night was the perfect alibi. You worry too much, hermano."

"The problem is you don't worry enough. I gotta be careful for the both of us."

"D, I mean, he's not that guy on T.V. in the brown coat who can solve a 20-year-old murder because he found a toothbrush... What's his name?"

He thought for a minute and replied "Colombo?"

"Colombo? No. What the fuck? How old are you?"

"What? What's wrong with watching Colombo?" Donovan laughingly asked.

"Nothing's wrong with watching Colombo if you still own a rotary phone, but here in the future, where we have the internet, that's not who I'm talking about," Rico said as he laughed at his friend's expense.

Shrugging his shoulders, Donovan replied, "He wears a brown coat. He solves crimes. How is this not the guy you're talking about?"

"Nah, not Colombo, grandpa. His coat is 80's brown."

"It's a brown coat, and what the hell is 80's brown?"

"He's not the guy. The other one. You know the one who is always turning his head to the side."

"From Law and Order? Goren?"

"No, the other guy. He keeps turning his head. He touches light bulbs. He's a germaphobe."

"Oh, Monk."

"Yeah! Monk. Now, if that cop was Monk, we would need to go to the precinct. Because he would've tied that shit together with a cracked eggshell he found near a dumpster or some shit. But, he's just a regular cop so we're in the clear."

"Ok, Rosey, the eternal optimist, but if he's walking my ass though a lineup tomorrow, I'll remember that you said he was just a regular cop." Donovan said in agreement with Rico's assessment of the situation.

"Then I guess we're in the clear... as long as Carlos don't do nothing stupid betwee—"

"You again, Negative Nancy. I told you I'll handle it."

"I'm just saying I know how it got past you, but how did it get past Slim?" Donovan asked.

Rico's eyes narrowed as he answered, "See, I'm gonna take that shade you just threw my way and turn it into sunshine because I'm an optimistic person. Otherwise, I'd shoot you in your kneecap."

"You know what I mean. Slim is all about no outsiders."

"It's different on the inside, hermano. Time slows down, and you're with one guy 22 hours a day, every day, with nothing else to do but get to know each other or kill each other. Hell, when we were on the inside, K.T., Slim, Carlos, and I ran the joint. We were the big bad wolves."

"Well, point is, y'all lil experiment didn't work."

"Whatever, ese, but let's switch gears to those monomaniacs we met last night. You gonna hit up… What'd you call her... Babygirl?"

Donovan lit a cigarette, took a long drag, and handed Rico the pack. After he exhaled, he responded. "I thought about it."

No sooner than he said the words did Rico laugh.

"What are you talking about? You thought about it? We almost went to jail over it. You should've seen yourself last night, looking like you were on a Carl Thomas video."

Donovan laughed as Rico sang the words of Carl Thomas' hit song *Emotional*.

"Whatever, Rosey. She helped us out in the clutch, which is more than what I can say about your boy who got us in this mess."

"Probably doesn't hurt she's drop-dead gorgeous."

Donovan chuckled. "She's pretty easy on the eyes."

"And pretty thick in the thighs."

"Ha, funny, but what did you think about her?"

Rico's eyes lit up as he responded. "Shit, I think that any chick that can professionally say fuck the police and won't give you her name until you go on your first date is a bad motherfucker."

"Date? Nah, Rosey, I'm—"

"Mijo, please. If you show up today, you're on a date. Hell, come to think about it, Donovan Brown out in daylight after the night we had. I mean... Hermano, she didn't even tell you the fucking *location* of your actual date. She told your black ass to find her on some, *Where in the World is Carmen San Diego* shit, and you're out here looking like you work for ACME Detective Agency. That's boss shit. Hell, the more I think about it, she's probably too good for you."

"Rico, I'll shoot you in your damn leg if you don't quit playing with me. Everybody from the south side knows, matter-of-fact, everyone in Houston knows, Frenchy's Chicken is the only spot that serves a king's special."

"That might be true, but it was brutal to watch. The way she had you standing there smiling like your black ass wasn't 26 seconds from life without parole. Ay, Dios mío. Like from an O.G.'s perspective, you're 'bout to drive twenty minutes out of your way *hoping* to buy this chick a king's special for the opportunity to what? Get her name? I mean, I'm just saying, sounds like some sucker shit to me."

Donovan responded jokingly, "And what would they call you? Carrying her girl Amanda to the car?"

"A beast, because, unlike you, my friend, that pussy has already been tested and tasted."

Donovan stopped looking at the house and turned to his friend. "You lying mother—"

"I have receipts."

Rico pulled out his phone and showed Donovan a picture of Amanda and him naked in bed. Donovan snatched the phone to examine it closer. He then looked back at his friend, stunned by the revelation.

"Wait, a damn minute! We spent all last night putting that linebacker in the ground. When did you—"

"'Bout two hours ago, homie. I took a shower, called her up, and the next thing you know, we were in pound town."

Donovan shook his head.

"Are you serious right now?"

"Hey man, what can I say? I'm half Colombian, and she's Dominican. We fuck like rabbits. Shit was good too. Kitty tasted like mangoes."

Donovan rubbed both hands across his face. He took another drag of his cigarette and said, "Un-fucking believable."

"I'm serious, D. It was exquisite, homie. Matter fact, I'm gonna go back soon as we're done with this shit. Cause when I tell—"

"There's Mel."

The man they were looking for was pointed out by Donovan. Shady Mel, the owner of a nightclub that held illicit gambling in the back. He'd been robbed more than once recently and had come to Donovan and Rico for protection, a bill he had not made good on yet. The pair got out of the car and walked across the street to meet the portly dark-skinned man walking down his driveway with a taller woman who was also similar in complexion.

"Yo, Shady," Donovan barked as the man stopped in his tracks and turned around. Donovan could tell by the shakiness in the man's voice that he was nervous as he responded.

"He... hey... D. What's good with you?"

Donovan walked up to the fidgeting man. He nodded his head and responded, "I mean, you tell me. We went by the shop and nobody was there with our check. Today is payday, so me and Rico decided to pay you a house visit."

"You didn't have to do that. I was gonna reach out after I got home."

"Well, we saved you the time."

"And I appreciate that... It's just I got raided by H.P.D. about a week ago, and they shut me down. I had to post bail, pay a lawyer, and a bunch of fines. My funds are a bit tight after all that. Especially with the downturn in the economy, you understand, right? This is what they call a market fluctuation."

Donovan nodded as Mel continued to speak, and he looked over at Rico, who was also nodding in agreement with what was being said. Donovan continued to bob his head solidly and responded.

"Market fluctuation...Right."

"See, D, you get it. I was just telling my girl how much vision you have. You see the big picture. Downturns in the economy and whatnot. But it won't last forever. Soon as I get on my feet, I got you."

As Mel was talking, Donovan was examining his platinum necklace that had 5 diamonds resting on the pendant. It was eye-catching yet elegant.

Mel noticed Donovan was looking at the necklace and said, "Oh, you like this. Yeah, man, my lady got this for me a while ago. Got some sentimental value to it, you know?"

"Yeah... Sentimental value. That's cool. What's the real value?"

"Huh?"

"I'm not big on sentiment. What's the real value?"

Donovan watched as Shady Mel nervously processed his words before responding.

"Oh, man, I... haven't checked in a while. It's kind of... an heirloom."

"I'll find out for you."

"Oh, man, you ain't gotta do that. I can—"

"I'll find out for you."

Donovan extended his hand as Shady Mel started reluctantly unclasping the necklace.

"Clasp is stuck. I can't seem to get it off."

"Do you need help?"

"Yeah, man, do you need help?" Rico said, stepping closer to the conversation. The message was obvious.

"Nah, nah, it's all good. It's coming off now."

Shady Mel took the necklace off and gave it to Donovan, who looked at it, smiled, and promptly put it around his neck.

Rico stepped closer and put his hand on the man's other shoulder. "This is why you gotta pay your bills on time, Mel. If your coverage was up to date, do you think I would've let a man rob you for your necklace in broad daylight, in front of your lady, leaving you looking like a sucker? Hell no! Cause when I say I got you, I got you. This kind of thing would've never happened with one of us around. You'd still have your chain and maybe, just maybe, her respect. Now you just look like a sucker who got his shit taken. But I'll leave you two alone. You seem like you got a lot on ya mind. Let's just hope they solve those market fluctuations by Friday."

"Yeah, you're right. I don't know what I was thinking... I'll have your bread by Friday," Mel said, demoralized by the encounter.

Donovan nodded in agreement and turned to leave, but Rico turned back and pointed towards Mel.

"Oh, speaking of dates, Mel. Give me 100 dollars cause this guy over here finally has a date, and you know... he can't show up empty-handed."

Donovan shook his head and chuckled as Mel, clearly embarrassed by the entire ordeal, gingerly handed the money over to Rico, and they all went their separate ways. Rico stopped Donovan as he got back in the car.

"You know I'm keeping that 100, right?"

6
JUNE 27TH

"*3*:37, I made good time," Donovan said as he parked his SUV in the University of Houston's parking lot. He thought about Rico's words and decided he'd smoke a cigarette before he went to *simp* on this woman he didn't know. As he lit the Camel cigarette, he replayed his friend's words over in his head. *Damn, what am I doing here?* he thought to himself.

"Ah hell. I'm hungry anyways," he said aloud. He was satisfied that even if she wasn't there, a meal from Frenchy's was worth the trip. He put out the cigarette he had just lit, got out of the car and headed toward the restaurant. The blistering Texas heat rushed over him like a blazing inferno. "Damn, it's hot," he said as he waited for his eyes to adjust to the sunlight. Being a native of the city, the Texas heat was something he was accustomed to, but today was unusually hot. It could've been the freshly tarred parking lot that was capturing the heat or the humidity, but either way, he was already regretting the location of their would-be date, considering the entire fast-food restaurant was an outdoor covered patio with no AC.

When he got inside, he was relieved it was slightly cooler, even if only a little. He scanned the area to see if she was there. Realizing she wasn't there created slight apprehension about seeing Rico if she didn't show. He knew his friend would never let him hear the end of it. As he finished scanning all the faces in the room, he realized she wasn't among them. The reality hit him, and as his doubt grew into slight embarrassment. He thought maybe he was the punchline to her joke of the night, and that he had imagined the chemistry he felt with her. He was no longer in the mood to eat southern fried chicken, no matter how good it smelled. As he was about to leave, he heard a familiar voice.

"Nichelle. My name is Nichelle Myers."

Donovan turned around. She looked even more attractive than she had the night before. She was wearing a yellow summer dress that clung to her athletic frame. His appetite for all things came back to him. He walked over and gave her a hug.

"So, I finally got a name."

"Not used to working for it, are you?"

Donovan chuckled. Her responses were something he was growing to appreciate in their short time getting acquainted.

"Only for things that matter."

"I should feel honored then."

"Well, it's nice to meet you, Nichelle," he said with a grin.

She smirked as well while looking up at him. "You mean without the police or my crazy ex-boyfriend showing up?" she said with the flair that had excited him over the last day or so.

"Yeah, without that. What's up with you two, anyway?"

"Food first, drama later."

"Wouldn't have it any other way," Donovan said as he smiled and nodded in agreement.

Nichelle walked past him towards the counter. He examined her supple bottom as it paraded to the front of the counter. *Damn, she got a fat ass*, he thought to himself. He joined her at the counter as she turned to him.

"What do you want? It's my treat."

The gesture surprised him, something she immediately picked up on.

"Oh please, the least I can do is get you some fried chicken. Besides, this is your money I'm using, anyway," she said jokingly.

The pair laughed as they stood in line to both get the King's special, a combination of 5 wings, Frenchy's famous dirty rice, and a fountain drink. It was the most common thing on the menu that everyone ordered, from the college kids to the members of the nearby church, to the people from the surrounding neighborhood. Frenchy's was a cornerstone of the community.

Donovan sat down at one of the teal wooden benches on the shaded patio. It wasn't long before Nichelle joined him, and the pair ate. Donovan enjoyed Nichelle's candor. To his eyes, she wasn't just sexy. He could find sexy anywhere, but her audaciousness was refreshingly authentic. From what he could gauge, she didn't fake the funk but enjoyed playing the game, and it was up to you to figure out which was which. Still, he had questions about the night before, and he was certain she did as well. He asked his question first.

"So, what's up with you and old boy from last night?"

"Lord, don't get me started," Nichelle replied as she took a long sip of her sweetened iced tea. After a spell, she let out a giant sigh.

"I met Bryan sophomore year of college. He plays, well, played football for the University of Houston as a tailback. He seemed decent enough at first, and for a while, things were good, but when he got hurt midway through our junior year, he took it hard. I think he felt like his shot at getting to the NFL was slipping away, which I kind of understood because football is all he's ever known, but he handled it poorly. He started drinking hard. I tried to be supportive at first, but the more I did, the worse he got. He just started getting clingy and controlling. He never wanted me to go anywhere or do anything... You know when they say misery loves company? That shit is so real. You don't even know."

Donovan watched as she started to fidget. He could tell by her matter-of-fact tone she was over the guy, but she was also reliving a past she wanted to put behind her. She needed to get this off of her chest. Understanding this, he sat quietly as she continued.

"By the time the new season started, in my mind, we had run our course. He had been drinking pretty heavily while he wasn't playing, and then he started missing rehab. About a week ago, I'd had enough. I told him that I needed some space and that he should focus on football. I needed to focus on school. I'm a marketing major, and I'm really trying to get an internship at Burrows Industries, so I didn't need that kind of distraction. Once I told him how I felt, he went ballistic. Starts off by saying everyone is turning their back on him, and why am I treating him like this? Then he says I'm the one who put his football career in jeopardy. Mind you, he's showing up to practice with vodka in a water bottle and drinking at least a pint of Hennessy every night, so how he thought that was gonna translate on the field, I'll never know. I didn't say anything, though. I just let him get it all out of his system. But then, he accuses me of sleeping around and tells me if he finds out I've cheated on him, it's not gonna end well. As he's saying it, he's standing over me, looking at me in a way he's never done before, and Bryan is a big guy."

"Damn, I'm sorry to hear that. I could tell last night something was going on, but you try to stay out of people's business. That had to be scary for you."

"Well... I wasn't scared or anything. I just didn't recognize the person in front of me. So, I told him, calmly, I've never cheated on him, and he's drunk, so he should go home to get some rest. He eventually calmed down, and I think he thought things were gonna go back to normal, but I was super done. The next morning, he calls me to apologize for how he'd handled himself. Once again, I didn't say a word. I let him get it all out of his system. Only difference was, this time, I was sitting in the football coach's office and let him hear everything he had to say. By the end of the day, they'd kicked him off the team and removed him from campus. He was pissed. He spent the day looking for me, blowing up my phone, and calling me all kinds of names, so I blocked his number... When you met him last night, that was the first time I'd seen him since everything happened."

Donovan nodded, processing the story. He'd become an expert judge of human reactions. Looking at her, he could tell by her distant look she was still very anxious about the entire ordeal, so he changed the subject.

"So, how long have you been going to Harvard?"

Nichelle laughed at the statement. "I've been in school for three years, and it's not Harvard; it's the University of Houston. But, I'm not telling you anything you don't know, so let me tell you something you may not know. We Cougars are just as real about our school as anybody who went to an HBCU."

"Alright, I feel you. My bad," he said half-jokingly as Nichelle took one of his fries and rolled her eyes, mocking him.

"Yeah, you feel me alright. I bet you wouldn't try that shit if I went to TSU or Prairie View."

"You probably right, but why didn't you?" he asked as he moved his fries away from her as she tried to take a few more. He gazed into her dark brown eyes with a slight grin.

"Why didn't I do what?"

"Go to an HBCU. There's one right across the street." Donovan answered as Nichelle gingerly reached for his fries again. He extended them to her, letting her pick a few up. After eating them, she responded.

"I wanted to go to Texas Southern, but the truth is, I'm going into oil and gas, and in this city, the University of Houston is considered the 4th best school to go to, let alone an HBCU, let alone TSU."

"Damn, I didn't think that kind of shit mattered much, but it makes sense now that you say it. I guess I thou—"

"Mayne, hold up. What in the hell do we have here?" His Houston drawl was unmistakable, and Donovan half chuckled as he looked at Nichelle, who had also recognized the voice. His best friend had showed up, along with Nichelle's friend Amanda.

"What are you doing here, Rosey?"

Rico chuckled as he sat on the bench across from his friend, swiping a few of the French fries from his now all but gone pile.

"I was trying to get a front-row seat to this love connection you're having. Besides, this one right here wanted some food and fluids before going for round five," Rosey said, sticking his tongue out to add unique emphasis to his point. His bluntness caught everyone but Donovan off guard.

"Well, I just lost my damn appetite," Donovan said as Rico grabbed one of his wings and proceeded to make himself comfortable sitting next to Nichelle.

"Don't knock it till you try it, right Amanda?" Rico looked over at the woman whose hand he was holding. Her grin said it all. Rico turned back towards the table as Amanda sat on the opposite side of him.

"Aw now, she's being all shy and shit. It's all good, mama. But enough about us, how's first base going?"

"First base? Please, he's still at home," Nichelle chimed in.

Donovan closed his eyes, bracing for his friend's reaction.

"Wait, please tell me he's still not trying to figure out your name."

"Nah, I finally told him."

"Good, 'cause you know I couldn't keep it from my boy too much longer."

Donovan's eyes bulged. "Wait a damn minute, Rosey. You mean to tell me you knew her name and didn't tell me?"

"Yeah, me and Nichelle go way back. But her friends, like me, call her Neecie," Rico said, causing the two to laugh.

Donovan realized he must have met her earlier when he was over at their place with Amanda, and smirked as the table laughed.

"So that's your nickname? Neecie?"

"One of them, but you can't call me that; we're not friends."

The two laughed as Donovan glanced over at Amanda, who shook her head in embarrassment and chuckled at his expense as well. After a few moments, Donovan couldn't help but join in. Rico responded.

"I like this one, D."

"Rico! Time and place, bruh." Donovan said to his best friend, who smiled a devilish grin. He knew he never knew when to quit, and was egging him on. Still, he was truly trying to get to know the woman, and now he was dealing with his best friend's unwanted intrusion. His friend's joke had run its course.

"Am I ruining your date, D?"

"Kinda, bro."

"So, you admit it, you're on a date!"

"Wait, we're on a date?" Nichelle chimed in, surprised by the statement.

"Well, I... um, what?"

His hesitation was all that Rico needed.

"Oh, man, I can't wait to get back to the hood and tell the fellas Donovan Brown is out here on a date stammering."

"Rico!"

"Alright. Alright, my bad, ese," Rico said, standing up and taking a deep bow towards Nichelle.

"The views and expressions on the Rico Show do not reflect Mr. Brown in any way, shape, or form. I am deeply sorry for any inconvenience this may have caused," Rico laughingly said. "Let's roll, Amanda."

The two walked through the door and disappeared out of sight. Donovan was flustered and tried to focus on Nichelle again, who was giggling.

"What?"

"Your brother is—"

"An ass."

"I was gonna say funny."

"Yeah, like the third wheel on a bicycle. I'm still tripping 'cause he knew your name. We were just kicking it earlier... So, if I'm not your friend, what should I call you?"

"I like Babygirl. It feels natural coming from you."

"Then I won't mess up a good thing."

The pair smiled at one another. Suddenly, Babygirl's smile went from a grin to concern.

"Donovan, look outside," Nichelle interjected abruptly.

He could tell something had slightly alarmed her. He turned around and could see his friend across the street being surrounded by three men.

"Hold on, Babygirl, I'll be right back."

"What? Wait!"

Donovan stood up and headed towards Rico, who was already losing his cool. He shouted at his friend to get his attention.

"Yo, Rico! You good?"

"I'm straight, brother. Just dealing with a bunch of clowns who are about to find out the hard way this ain't the circus."

One man stepped closer to Rico so they were eye to eye.

"Hey, what you say, motherfucker?" the man snarled.

Donovan stepped in between the two men and pulled out his .45 caliber Smith & Wesson pistol, and cocked it, forcing the three men to collectively step back and lift their hands in the air. He looked at the man in front of him, who was now clearly nervous, and said, "Look, all I know is if my brother ain't good, then I ain't good. And if I ain't good, then I'm gonna make sure we all have a bad day. Cause you know... misery loves company and shit like that. So, I'm gonna ask again. Is everyone good?" Donovan gripped his pistol tightly. Looking for any reaction from the three men.

The man in front said, "Nah, patna...we good...my man... just a misunderstanding, that's all."

"See, here's the problem with misunderstandings; they can be costly. So, I'm gonna need y'all to run them pockets to make this day a little better."

"Man, we ain't gon—"

Donovan put the gun directly underneath the man's chin interrupting his response.

"Fool, you must got me confused with a man that repeats himself. Now run them pockets or keep the money, but I promise where you'll be going next, you won't need it, anyway."

Donovan scanned the men carefully. He nodded his head as Rico walked over to take the wallets of the men, who were now nervously compliant. He could see the fear in their eyes. He also saw Nichelle walking up, watching him holding the pistol and keeping her distance, looking somewhat embarrassed by his actions. *Fuck*, he thought to himself, convinced that he had just blown any chance of the rest of the night going well. The man in front of him, along with his companions, all offered their wallets for their lives. He glanced over at Rico, who nodded again to confirm things were in order.

"Ok, now we're good. Why don't you boys run along while you still can and enjoy the rest of your day?"

The men backed up and ran off at a full sprint as Donovan put the pistol back into his waistband after they disappeared out of sight. He looked at Nichelle, who appeared distraught. He wasn't sure what to say.

"Hey Babygirl... um... Look, I just want to sa—"

"Can you take me home please?" Nichelle said abruptly.

"Yeah... um... My car is right... right over there."

7
SAY MY NAME

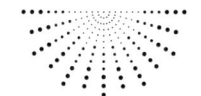

Fucking Rico, man, always into somethin', he thought to himself. His date with Nichelle, however short-lived, had come to an abrupt end, and while he wanted to address it with her, he knew there was no point talking about it. He was fortunate she was allowing him to take her home at all. He looked over at her sun dress and the way it clung to her thick thighs. *Damn*, he thought to himself. Despite the chemistry he felt, he had missed a chance to get to know her. He knew pulling a gun on a date meant the end of the date. *It's all good. You win some; you lose some.*

"My building is here on the right," she said. The student condominiums were close to campus. He parked on the road and said nothing as she was about to exit the vehicle. She looked back as she opened the door.

"What do you do for a living?"

Donovan looked her in the eyes and asked in his grizzly voice.

"Do you want a pretty lie or the ugly truth?"

"I want... um... You know what? It was nice meeting you. Have a good day." She was about to exit the car when Donovan gently touched her hand.

"Look I just... I'm a good dude, but I'm a street dude, and where I'm from, it's hunt or be hunted."

"I get that, Donovan. It's just… I'm already dealing with my crazy ex, and I just want to feel safe. You feel me?"

"I can understand that. I do. And I can promise you that you will never feel unsafe with me. I didn't go to college. I live in the real world, and the real world has guns in it."

"But you robbed those people in broad daylight, D."

"It wasn't about the money, Babygirl. I live by a code. Where I come from, you gotta send a message. I'm sorry if that made you feel uncomfortable, but anytime I see someone being taken advantage of, I'm gonna stand up for them."

"The way you looked out for me last night... You're a protector."

Her eyes met his as two souls meet when the truth is present. He watched her as she processed his words, looked away, and then reestablished eye contact in a more analytical way.

"Look, I really like you, and if I'm being honest with you, the gun doesn't bother me so much. It's just... It's this drama with my ex and… I don't want my life to be too complicated."

"I feel you. You gotta do what's best for you, but you also need to have fun. Look, all I want to do is to get to know you, make you laugh, and—"

"Fuck on me some?"

Donovan smirked and reiterated his earlier question, "Do you want a pretty lie or the ugly truth?"

Stunned by his response, she replied, "Ok, I'll bite. What's the ugly truth?"

"I wanna fuck the shit out of you. But, not as bad as you wanna fuck me."

"You cocky motherfucker. What is that supposed to mean?" Nichelle asked.

"Well, look at the evidence. In the last twenty-four hours, you've seen me knock a man unconscious, get hemmed up by the police, and rob a man in broad daylight, and the first thing you ask after all of that is 'can you take me home?' I'm not sayin' either of us wants it today, but you damn sure want to know which pistol I'm packing is bigger."

"Don't presume to know me, you cocky motherfucker."

She leaned in and kissed him feverishly. Taking his hand and pressing it firmly against her breast. With his other hand, he grabbed her ass cheek and squeezed it tightly. As he moved his lips from hers and onto her neck, she moaned in ecstasy. She reached for his cock and gripped it tightly. Instinctively, he slid his hand toward her panty line, which she welcomed as she opened her legs to allow him access. He pressed his fingertips against her yellow panties that had become moist with her nectar. She squeezed his dick harder and fiddled with the zipper when suddenly she pushed away from him.

"Damn it! Why am I like this? "She muttered to herself.

Donovan, still aroused, took a breath to calm himself.

Nichelle looked at him, "Ahem. That was a mistake, and you're wrong about everything you just said and… Um… Yeah… Whew, goodnight." She nodded awkwardly and composed herself to get out of the car.

Donovan leaned his head back against the headrest and sighed. As he closed his eyes, he heard a knock on the widow. He rolled the window down, and Nichelle leaned in.

"And for the record, the gun is definitely bigger."

She cut her eyes, a retaliatory response for his prior honesty, turned around, and walked off into the distance beyond the gate.

Donovan wanted to pursue her but had to pause to calm his erection. When he had finally calmed himself, he got out of the car and trotted towards the gate, neatly catching it as a resident was leaving. He walked into the complex and saw Nichelle several paces away. He also noticed someone gaining ground on Nichelle from an adjacent angle.

"Bryan," he muttered.

Her disgruntled ex from the night before was already hovering over Nichelle when Donovan arrived.

"Leave me the hell alone, Bryan. I said it's over," Nichelle yelled. As she walked away, he snatched her arm.

"You stupid bitch, you don't tell me when it's over. I tell you, and it ain't never over."

"Then I'm telling you for her. It's over," Donovan said, walking up to the situation.

Bryan released her arm and turned towards him, glaring hotly, his eyes full of anger. He started walking toward Donovan, who never broke his stride, ready to meet this confrontation head-on. Bryan pointed and yelled furiously.

"Hey motherfucker, I'm talking to *my* bitch. You better back the fu—"

Donovan swiftly grabbed Bryan by his shirt collar and shoved him against the wall. He pressed his elbow against the man's larynx, cutting off his oxygen, and put his pistol to the temple of his head, forcing all the anger in the man's eyes to flee. With cold, calculative conviction, Donovan spoke.

"Now, maybe you're dumb, maybe you got a death wish, or maybe you just been able to get away with all the fuckboy shit fuckboys get away with 'cause nobody is around to check you otherwise. But this right here... This right here would be the wrong place at the wrong time, and I'm definitely the wrong one. So, the question you gotta ask yourself is, is she worth dying for when she clearly doesn't want your bitch ass anymore? You feel me, Bryan?"

Beads of sweat poured from his forehead as his silence revealed all that Donovan needed to understand. What had replaced the anger he'd previously seen in Bryan's eyes was fear. It was the same fear he'd seen the night before when he had put an end to Adrian Watson's life.

"Look, man... I don't want no trouble," Bryan said calmly.

"Nah, you want trouble. You just don't want it with someone your own size, but here we are. So I'm gonna need your wallet, Bryan."

"M...my wallet?"

"Just so you know, I keeps a hollow point in the chamber, so you decide. You want me to use my trigger hand or my free hand to take your wallet?"

"Ok, ok, chill."

Bryan nervously pulled out his wallet and handed it over to Donovan. Still aiming the gun, he removed his hand from Bryan's throat, taking the wallet and examining its contents.

"Bryan Scruggs. 2348 Tierwester Street... you're over there by OST and Scott... by that Taco Bell."

The man muffled something inaudible.

"What did you say? Speak up."

The man mumbled again, louder this time, allowing Donovan to make out the words.

"Oh, this is your mama's address. That's real useful... Saves me the hassle of having to go find her if we need to have a chat. 'Cause uh... I wasn't the best student, but I picked up on math pretty good. I like the part where you have to do both sides of the equation. You feel me? So, for instance, if anything ever was to happen to Babygirl right here, then I got no choice but to make the same thing happen to Mrs. Scruggs. You feel me, Bryan? And before you go off thinking about being a hero, just remember how powerless you are right at this moment. Now, here's your wallet, minus the 500 that was in it 'cause you know, anytime you pull a gun, there's an un-holster surcharge, a re-holster tax, and a cleaning fee... I'm sure you know. You college boys know all about inflation. I mean, unless you want me to use it, then, well, you won't need the money anyway. So, I guess what I'm saying is, get the fuck out of here before things get real complicated for all of us."

He watched carefully as Bryan backed up slowly and then scrambled to the exit of the complex once he felt he was an appropriate distance away from being shot.

Donovan turned around to Nichelle, who was standing there looking at him. He wasn't sure how to respond. He put the gun up and apologized.

"Look, Babygirl, I didn't mean to—"

"Shut up and kiss me."

She leaned into him and kissed him with a passion that blazed hotter than the kiss from the night before. He pulled her closer as the kiss reached its peak, but she pulled away from him, leaving him both excited and confused. He looked at her as she looked at him, wanting to re-engage. After a spell, she finally spoke.

"You want to come inside?"

Suppressing his grin, he nodded.

The pair walked to her door to enter the apartment.

As the door closed, he picked her up and kissed her intensely. His dick was throbbing against his pants, something he made sure she felt as he pressed it firmly against her pelvic bone. He moved his lips onto the side of her neck and gently sunk his teeth into her flesh, causing her to squirm in ecstasy.

"Oh shit."

She moved as she used her hand to press his face deeper into her neck, showing she wanted more, to which he gladly obliged. He bit a little more aggressively, forcing her to moan at the pleasure of his intensity.

"Enough of this."

He carried her into the back of the apartment without hesitation.

"It's the room on the left," she said.

Donovan obeyed and walked into the room and laid her on the top of the cream goose-down comforter on her queen-sized bed. He licked her on the side of her neck as she moaned, planting her nails deep into his back. Next, he helped her out of her dress as she worked on her bra to expose her shapely c-cup breasts sitting naturally against her frame. He viciously attacked her left areola with a passion that forced her back onto her back as she moaned.

"Oh shit. What... What are you doing to me?"

She pushed his head over to the right breast as he bit her with intensity. The cocktail of pain and pleasure he was providing turned her on as she moaned again. He released her nipple, sat up, and took a seat on the bed, pulling off his clothes. His dick was at full attention. He watched Nichelle, eyes widened, fixated on his package. She lifted her eyes to look at him and then back to his package.

"Remember when I said your pistol was bigger?"

"Yeah."

"I lied."

"Oh, I know."

Donovan smirked as he resumed kissing her on her breast, placing his lips on her caramel-colored nipple as she moaned in pleasure. Without provocation, she wrapped her hands around his cock and stroked it, making it harder. He leaned into her as his deep brown dick throbbed in her hand as if it had a life of its own. He removed her panties, and he looked at her. She was undeniably beautiful. She was sexy, and he was ready to enter her.

"Put it in me," she whispered lustfully.

He gladly obliged.

"Oh, shit," they moaned simultaneously, feeling their mutual gratification. Donovan could feel her wetness saturating his dick.

"Wait, slow down... I've never had anyone this big before," She panted as he looked into her eyes.

"Damn, this is tight, Babygirl."

He slowly pushed his way through the tightness of her walls, watching her eyes roll with each inch inserted.

"Don't worry, I'm gonna take it slow," he said.

He took his dense cock and slid it a little deeper into her.

"Oh, my God." She wailed as her body opened up. He could feel the heat of her pussy pulsating against his dick. With each stroke, he intensified his desire. She arched her back as he pushed into her, grabbing her by the ass.

"Oh, is that how you want it? You want me to fuck you?" he asked rhetorically. He pushed into her harder with each stroke, his dick becoming more saturated with her moisture.

"Oh, shit, if you gonna fuck me, then fuck me then," she moaned.

It was all the permission he needed. He began to savagely pump his dick into her, hitting the back of her walls with each thrust. She released a high pitched squeal of pleasure, turning him on even more. His dick swelled as her tight pussy clasped around every bit of his 10-inch cock.

"Give me that dick, daddy!" she yelled lustfully as her breasts bounced in a rhythmically beautiful motion to each thrust. He propped her legs on his bulging shoulders and bit at her calf muscle as he stroked her, pulling all but the tip of his dick out with each stroke and thrusting it forcefully.

"I'm cumming!" Nichelle squealed as she took her hands and dug them into the muscle of his back as he pushed into her.

"Let it go, Babygirl," he moaned as she released her nectar, making her pussy too wet for him to last much longer.

"Oh, shit!" he growled.

It was his turn to release his orgasm. He viciously clapped against her walls as his orgasm rushed through his entire body. Collectively, they were done. Donovan fell on top of her. He was still inside her with no strength to move. He took two heavy breaths and, with what strength the air gave him, exited her body before collapsing next to her on the bed.

"That... was... incredible," she moaned, still shivering from the experience.

Donovan reached for his pants and lit a cigarette which Nichelle promptly snatched from him. He looked at her. She undid the clasp of his newly acquired necklace and put it around her own neck.

"How does it look?" she asked playfully.

He pulled her into his lean, muscular arms and replied, "It looks like... I just got robbed."

8
STRAIGHT GANGSTERISM

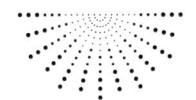

A Year Later

"THAT'S IT, BABY! FUCK ME LIKE YOU MISS ME!"

Nichelle tightened the walls of her pussy, forcing his dick to release the euphoric orgasm he'd been building over the last thirty minutes. Donovan continued to cum and became hyper-sensitive as Nichelle contracted her wall muscles to apply pressure to his already sensitive dick. He could not take anymore. He fell next to Nichelle, resting gently on her shoulder, as she struggled to catch her breath beside him.

"You are… I came eight times," she muttered out aloud.

He watched as her realization transformed into a jovial chuckle.

She looked back at him and continued, "Do you…have any…idea what it feels like to cum that hard that many times?" She laughed again.

Donovan watched her as she touched her crotch area as if to protect it.

"Oh, my God. I love you," she said, panting and wheezing.

"Are you talking to me or him?"

"Oh, definitely him. You're a'ight," she laughingly panted.

Satisfied by her reaction, he slapped her on her left ass cheek, fully exposed to the sunlight. The two laughed out loud as Donovan attempted to light a cigarette, which prompted Nichelle to snatch it out of his hand. He watched as she tossed it away from the bed towards the trash can, nearly missing. Donovan leaned into her and bit her on the shoulder playfully. She lightly slapped his face and chuckled as she rolled on top of him before gently reaching between his legs for his cock which was exhausted from their earlier session. She gently stroked it two times and smiled, never taking her eyes from his manhood.

"Besides, who wouldn't want that monster inside of them switching up their organs every day?"

"I don't even know who you are anymore. Just nasty."

The two got up and showered, which led to another lovemaking session. Eventually, Donovan got dressed to meet Rico, who was picking him up for a big moment. Donovan's brother Slim was being released from prison. As he put on his gray sweatpants, he could hear Nichelle opening the door for Rico.

"Hey, boo, where's my boy?" Donovan heard as he joined them at the front door.

"There he is, getting on my damn nerves," she responded.

Rico closed his eyes and asked what he really wanted to know. "How's Amanda doing?"

"Still not talking to you."

"I made one mistake, Neecie. Why can't she let it go?"

"Mistake? You fucked someone else in her room."

"A woman we both slept with before! Plus I asked permission."

"While she was dozing off."

"She was tired, and I was horny. I asked her for permission, and she said, 'whatever.' That's permission."

Donovan continued to listen as Nichelle waved her hands enthusiastically, rolled her eyes, responded to his last outburst.

"Rosey, you're too smart to be this stupid. 'Can I have your piece of cake?' is something you ask for when a person is half awake. 'Can I fuck someone else in your apartment while you're sleeping?' is definitely something you want to make sure the person you're asking is fully coherent for."

"Ay, Dios mío, she drives me crazy. Just tell her to answer my calls. Ok?"

"Rico, she's not gonn —"

"Please, Neecie. She's my wildflower. I need her. I'm gonna go crazy if I—"

"Fine, Rosey. I'll talk to her... I got you."

"My girl! Thank you, mamacita," Rico said excitedly.

"If y'all done ruining Amanda's life, we should hit the road," Donovan interjected after eavesdropping on their conversation as he was getting ready.

Nichelle punched him in the arm playfully, "Whatever. You're excited to see your big brother."

"I'm just ready to get on the road, Babygirl."

"I wish I could go with you."

"Trust me, all Slim is gonna want to do is take an alcohol bath and call up one of his old ladies. Besides, there will be more than enough time in a few days at Mrs. Gladys' house. Thank you for sharing your party, by the way."

"Boy, hush. How could I pass up a graduation slash welcome home party? Especially if it means Mama G is gonna make her world-famous oxtails... she is making the oxtails, isn't she?"

"Ask her son." Donovan nodded in Rico's direction. Rico turned to Nichelle and smiled.

"Mamacita, for you, I'll kill the bull myself,"

Nichelle danced in place and replied, "Oh, I can't wait. Well, you all have a good time. I'm going to the mall to get a new outfit."

Donovan nodded and kissed her one last time. As the pair were about to head out, Nichelle stopped him.

"Baby, I need some money."

"What happened to the money I gave you yesterday?"

"That money was for yesterday. I need money for today."

Donovan checked his pockets to see how much he had on him and eventually pointed to a small pile of cash bundles stacked on top of the counter.

"Take that cash on the counter next to the Glock... and leave me a couple of stacks, could you?"

"I make no promises, my love," she said as she kissed him on the cheek again and pranced off.

"Babygirl, leave me two sta—"

"Y'all have a good day."

Donovan, recognizing he was losing this battle, waved his hand dismissively. As the two men headed out the door to get in the jet-black Tahoe SUV, Donovan could feel his best friend's gaze on the side of his face.

"What?"

"I see you still trickin' on this one, eh?"

"Leave me be with that, Rosey. I don't trick, I treat, especially when I'm treated well. Besides, she's different."

As they turned on the car and drove, Rico continued, "Look, she might be different, but here's something universal about women. You gotta keep up whatever you start, and in our line of work, that's probably not the best idea, is all I'm saying."

"Mind your own business, Rosey." The road trip was silent for a while after that statement but as the friends they are, they eventually started talking again.

The Texas Department of Corrections was about an hour away. Donovan hadn't seen his bother in over two years. Slim had taken the brunt of the robbery charges when he and Rico had gotten arrested for the heist they had been attempting. Since that time, Donovan had stepped up as the leader of their crew, simply known as, "The 713 Boyz," the first zip code in the Houston area.

When they got to the prison, they parked to wait for Slim to be released. Rico told jokes to pass the time while they waited.

Donovan couldn't sleep completely, but dozed, listening to his friend.

"D! Are you listening?"

"Rico, you been doin' this shit for 30 minutes. Can we just sit here, quietly without the stand-up co—"

"Come on, D, work with me. It passes the time, bro. Plus, this is good. I'm thinking about adding it to my routine."

Donovan let out an enormous sigh, and looked at his best friend, who had the expression of a kid on Christmas day, excited to open his first gift. He shook his head and relented.

"Shit. Fine, Rosey. What's the question?"

"Damn it, D! Pay attention."

"Just tell me the goddamn joke, Rico!" he said with a little shortness in his tone.

"Fine. I won't give you the setup to the joke, but here it is.... What do you call a *side bitch* with some wet ass pussy?"

Donovan took a drag of his cigarette and thought about it halfheartedly. After a spell, he exhaled the fumes and finally responded.

"Shit, man, I don't know. What do you call 'em, bruh?"

"Poseidon! You get it? Because it's wet, and the pussy is on the side. P-side-on."

Donovan looked at his best friend blankly. Silence filled the air. He didn't like the joke but he knew his friend wanted him to. After a second, he laughed.

"Holy shit. That one was funny, man."

"You damn right it was! Especially when chicks start saying shit like 'I got that Poseidon pussy!' Man, I'm telling you, Kevin Hart ain't seeing me in these comedic streets. I swear I was killing them in the joint with these jokes."

"I'm sure you were, Rico." Donovan responded convincingly enough to persuade his friend that he believed him. He didn't, but Rosey was always seeing things in their best possible light and he didn't want to be a raincloud. After a spell Rico continued.

"Amanda thinks I got a shot at a career in comedy. As soon as we get a big enough score, I'm gonna take some time and work on a routine and go to the Improv and work the circuit. That's my exit strategy."

"Comedy career? Bro, you serious right now?"

"What? It can't be worse than what we're doing right now. We can't do this shit forever, D."

He wasn't sure why the words stung but they did. Their rusted, jagged-edged truth serrated his reality. The streets were all he'd ever known. He'd never thought about leaving the street life. He'd never had a reason to, and he never knew that his friend wanted to leave them. Suddenly, the marginal joke became much larger in his mind.

"I didn't know you wanted to leave the game, Rico."

"Yeah... I've been talking to Amanda and—"

"Wait, I know you didn't just roast me about tricking on Nichelle, and you are out he—"

"Let me finish, ese. Me and Amanda will run our course one day. We're just having fun, and, if I'm honest with myself, she deserves better than what I am now. But what really got me thinking is I met the most amazing chick I've ever met, and the whole while she goes to school five Texas blocks up the road from a neighborhood I've lived in all my life. That got me thinking about what kind of women are in Dallas, what is the weather like in Chicago, or what's the best thing to eat in Columbia where my pops is from. I want to go and find out...I can't do that robbing people, but... I think I can do that in comedy. Nah... I know I can."

He'd rarely seen his friend this passionate, or serious about anything, which meant supporting him was important. There was no question about what he was going to say next.

"Alright, Rosey, when you make it, I'm your bodyguard. I got you."

Rico punched his friend in the arm playfully. "Nah, man, I'm gonna hire a Bruce Leroy-looking motherfucker to handle all that. I need you to watch the money. Be my manager."

Donovan took a drag of his cigarette and, after exhaling, replied, "You serious?"

"Dead-ass."

He took another drag of the cigarette and said, "I'm with it. If they screw us on the contract, we'll just rob the moth-"

"Yo, look! Is that him?"

Donovan looked over to the gates of the Huntsville Correctional Facility and smirked, shaking his head. "Yeah... That's him, alright." He tossed the remainder of his cigarette out of the window and flicked the lights of the car twice. A dark brown-skinned, burly man whose arms were covered in tattoos walked towards the car. He had a clean-shaven head and was wearing a white muscle shirt with black jeans. Even from the distance separating them, he noticed the multiple tattoos that had been added to Slim's six-foot-three frame since the last time he had seen him.

"Been a long time coming, huh?" Rico said.

"No doubt."

"The 713 Boyz are back."

"Yeah... We're back."

9
THE STRENGTH OF THE PACK IS THE WOLF

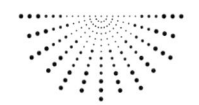

The pair exited the vehicle. Donovan leaned against the black Tahoe and smiled at his brother.

"What up, Slim?"

"Out on bail! Fresh outta jail! Trying to find some tail! On a woman with an ass that's as big as a whale's!" Slim yelled as he performed a local dance commonly known in Houston as "The South Side," which had been made famous by the rap posse knowns as *That Screwed-up Clique*. The other two men joined in with Slim in excitement.

"Welcome back, Slim."

"Rosey!" Slim barked in his deep grizzly voice as he play-fought with him.

The tall, wide-bodied man wrestled with Rico as Donovan chuckled. After a brief spell, Slim stopped.

"Alright, alright, let's get the fuck out of here before they come out here and try to lock my black ass up again for assaulting my ride home."

The men laughed, then hopped into the vehicle. As they drove,

Donovan felt settled. His brother was back in the fold, but Rico's words lingered with him.

We can't do this shit forever.

The words had hit Donovan like a megaton bomb. He had never considered doing anything else, and now it was all he could think about. What would life be like outside of the game?

The drive back was full of small talk and conversations about the inside. As they arrived back at the old neighborhood, Donovan glanced at his brother. His clean-shaven head and goatee were impeccable. He'd picked up a considerable amount of muscle since the last time he'd seen him too. He'd let him know his hard work had paid off.

"You look good, Slim."

"Ah! You know me, Chop. I'm gonna hit the weights when I'm in there. Bet that. Now all I'm tryin' to do is hit a piece of that Poseidon pussy."

"Wait a damn minute. You heard Rosey say that joke before?"

"Fool, I was there when he told it. He was killing them in the joint. He had the white gangs, the black gangs, the C.O., and the warden laughing. Hell, we used to get an extra hour of rec on Saturdays just so Rico could do his thing."

"I told you I was nice with these jokes," Rico interjected.

Donovan nodded in agreement and then turned his attention back to his brother.

"I see. It's good to have you back, bruh. I got you set up at Mama's house."

"And what about you?" Slim asked.

"Oh, D. He's staying with his girlfriend," Rico answered for him.

Donovan felt Slim punch the back of the car seat to show his surprise.

"Wait, Chop got a chick now?"

"Yeah, been about a year too."

"It ain't been no damn year, Rosey," Donovan grumbled.

"Yeah, it has been, hermano. The Texans just held a memorial for Adrian Watson."

"Oh, damn. They did, didn't they? It's been a year?"

As Donovan processed the words, Slim interjected, cutting both men off.

"Ok, so screw all that, though. What did you get her?"

Donovan shrugged his shoulders in response. "Nothin'... we don't do that kind of stuff. Besides, she's at the store buying stuff for herself right now."

He could feel the weight of his brother's hand on his shoulder.

"I'ma tell you somethin', brotha. Love... especially black love, is some beautiful shit. You gotta romance your hoe. Make her feel special, you know, take her out to eat and spend money on her, shit like that."

"Spending money ain't ever the problem. He's a whole magician, got a bag full of tricks," Rico interjected.

Donovan ignored both of them and responded, "Slim, did you just try to give me relationship advice on women while calling them hoes? Look y'all worry about y'all, and I'm gonna worry about mine. What me and Babygirl got is what me and Babygirl got."

"That's what I'm talkin' about, Chop! Protect your queen," Slim roared jokingly in his southern drawl.

Donovan flipped his brother off.

This back-and-forth banter between the three of them was enjoyable. His family together. Both brothers, one by blood, one by choice.

When they arrived at the house, he parted ways with Slim and headed back to his place to drop off Rico, whose words were still with him. He'd never imagined either of them getting out of the life, but since he'd met Nichelle, he looked forward to each new day. *Think about something else,* he told himself. He shifted his thoughts and landed on the lighter topic of not getting Nichelle anything for their one-year anniversary. He knew she got everything she wanted, whenever she wanted, but maybe his friends had a point. Should he have gotten something? He'd never been in a committed relationship. How could he possibly know what the rules were?

Man, fuck that, I'm good. Shit, she spent five thousand at the mall today. That's the anniversary gift... besides, if it was a big deal, then... she would've said something at some point, right? Yeah... I'm good.

The thought half convinced him out of his growing doubt. He looked at his friend, who knew what he was thinking.

"Rosey... you think I—"

"You screwed up big time, ese. Ladies dig any moment to feel special."

Damn, he thought to himself. Rico was right. *Well, if she doesn't bring it up. Neither will I.* He shrugged his shoulders, accepting his fate.

"Well, let me go hear this woman's voice," he said as he left the car.

He was about to open the door when it was flung open, and Nichelle greeted him with a passionate kiss.

"I just want to say I love you so much."

Donovan was startled. He wasn't sure what he'd done to deserve this kind of response, but he was relieved to have it.

Bark! Bark!

His focus went immediately to the sound coming from his home.

"Is that a..."

Bark! Bark!

There it was again.

Donovan walked in with intent, looked around, then paused, surprised by a rottweiler puppy.

"What in the hel—"

"Hell are you gonna name the puppy?" Rico interjected. He walked into the living room, making eye contact with Donovan as if to say, "Shut the fuck up."

Picking up on the cue, Donovan watched in silence as Nichelle lifted the puppy in the air, smiled, and snuggled with it. Never taking her eyes off the pup, she responded.

"I... I don't know, Rico. I haven't thought about it. How did you pull this off, Donovan Brown?"

"Well, for starters, he has me. See, he was telling me how this was you guy's anniversary and how you've always wanted a puppy because you never grew up with one, and my boy Carlos just had a litter of full-blooded Rottweilers. So, me and D went to pick this one out the other day, and this morning before I knocked on the door, I snuck the little guy into the backyard."

None of it was true, but all of it was working. Nichelle was jumping up and down with giddiness and grinning from ear to ear as she snuggled with the puppy.

Donovan, stunned by his best friend's thoughtfulness and quick thinking, nodded to show his appreciation. This was classic Rico. He enjoyed making people happy and finding opportunities to do so. As Nichelle came over to hug Donovan, he looked his best friend in the eye.

"Thank you," he mouthed.

Rico winked in return, and he knew it never needed to be mentioned again. Rico pointed to the pile of money that Nichelle had left on the counter and Donovan chuckled. Two thousand dollars was the price of the puppy. Donovan nodded in agreement. Rico took the cash, and Nichelle released the embrace to resume playing with her new-found playmate.

"You know what we gotta call him, right?" Donovan said.

"Of course. Our favorite movie, *Rocky*," she replied. She then turned to Rico. "I really appreciate you, Rosey, but you gotta go. The only people staying here are about to do freaky things to one another."

"Well, I don't mind if you don't," Rico said jokingly as Nichelle shoved him towards the door.

"Bye, boy," she said as she closed the door. She then turned her attention back to Donovan, her eyes full of lust. "Pull it out," she said, her voice dripping with seduction.

He smirked and walked over to her.

"Come here, you," she beckoned.

The two touched each other, wasting no time as she grabbed his jeans and began rubbing his crotch. He gently bit the side of her neck. He lifted her sports bra off of her body, exposing her breasts, and ran his tongue from her neck down to her right breast. He eventually settled on biting her left breast, yet not as hard as she liked. She pushed his face into her breast to show she wanted more. Still, he resisted. He wanted her to say the word.

"Harder," she whispered.

He obliged, digging his teeth into her flesh, forcing her to moan.

"More," she commanded.

He pulled back and looked at her lustfully. "Get on your knees," he commanded.

She smiled and complied with the exchange of power that had just taken place.

He unzipped his pants and pulled out his dick, which was growing in anticipation.

She looked up with seductive innocence and asked, "What do you want me to do with it?"

"I want you to take care of it."

Nichelle smiled, licked the palm of her right hand, and stroked the head of his now erect cock. The sensation flowed through his body. She then licked the palm of her left hand and placed it around the rest of his shaft. Her sensual nature had matured into full-blown lust. She looked up at him.

"You just gonna stand there, or are you gonna put it in my mouth?"

Without a word, he grabbed the back of her head and pressed his dick in between her open lips, causing her to moan as saliva dripped from their union. She sucked his rock-hard dick while using both hands to stroke him in a rhythmic motion.

"Oh, shit," he moaned as he continued to push her head deeper around his manhood. The sensation made his legs tremble as she slurped loudly, gagging on his 10-inch dick.

"I want to taste it."

Her words were muffled by the fact his cock was in her mouth, pulsating, building to climax.

"That's it, baby, suck that dick."

She persisted. Harder, faster, he could take no more.

"I'm... 'bout...to..."

His cum flowed into her mouth, and without hesitation, she continued to suck until he moaned savagely with satisfaction.

Donovan looked at her with quenched eyes, aware she wanted the same pleasure. He pushed her to the floor, pulled off the black tights she had on, and buried his face into her pussy.

"Baby... what... oh, God."

She moaned as he trapped her clit inside his lips, drowning it in an ocean of saliva and her nectar, which he couldn't swallow fast enough. He massaged her clit with his tongue, causing it to firm. He could feel the ridges of his tongue pressing against her soft flesh.

"Don't stop. Please, God, don't stop," she moaned.

He released her clit from its pleasure prison, letting the sensation of cool air mix with the heat and moisture of his tongue. She was losing control.

"Oh, shit, baby. Eat your pussy," she moaned.

He wrapped his lips around her clit again and pressed his tongue against it. The heat and moisture from his constant licking forcing her body to shake furiously.

"Oh, God... I'm... cumming," she squealed.

Her nectar saturated his chin as he continued to suck on her until she pushed his head away from her thighs.

He rested next to her, looking at her naked, shimmering body, now satisfied. He reached for his cigarettes from his pants, which were still hovering around his ankles, and pulled one out. He glanced over at Babygirl. She was still wearing the diamond pendant she had taken from him a year ago.

"I love you, D," she mumbled, fighting her impending slumber.

We can't do this shit forever.

Rico's words echoed in his mind. It all mattered. Getting out of the game mattered because she mattered. But life outside of the game? What did that look like? Whatever it would become, he knew he wanted her to be a part of it.

"I love you, Babygirl." He kissed her and put the cigarette back in the pack again.

10
THE STRENGTH OF THE WOLF IS THE PACK

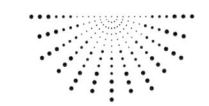

The cookout was just like he imagined it. The twinge of smoke brisket filled the air, whetting his appetite instantly. It hit Nichelle's appetite, too, as she promptly punched him in the arm after taking a large breath of air.

"Damn it, D! You did not tell me Rico was barbecuing! I'm out here trying to look cute in a crop top, knowing damn well I'm 'bout to go in on some ribs."

"Babygirl, you just said you wanted oxtails. That's as messy as they come—"

"I don't want to hear it. Look, you're gonna have to put some food to the side. I'm not gonna ugly eat in front of your brother when I ain't never met him."

"I'll see what I can do."

"You know everyone from the neighborhood loves Slim," Nichelle said as they entered the house.

Donovan shrugged. He knew his brother was always likable until he wasn't. If nothing else, he was respected. Donovan didn't like attention and didn't feel entirely comfortable bringing Babygirl around this element. In his mind, it was all too close for comfort. He approached his brother, who was talking to an almond-skinned man he'd never seen before.

"There's Chop!" Slim belted boisterously.

Donovan nodded as they approached.

"Yo, Chop, this is my boy K.T. We did time together. He's a hell of a wheelman."

K.T. turned towards Donovan, nodded, and the pair exchanged a handshake.

"And who do we have here?" Slim asked as he walked towards Nichelle, smiling and looking at her lips. "Damn, Rosey, you were right. She looks like a short Naomi Campbell." He turned to Donovan. "You did good, lil bro."

"Excuse me? I'm nobody's short Naomi Campbell," Nichelle belted defensively. "I'm more of a thick Nia Long."

Everyone laughed, but no one louder than Slim.

Donovan couldn't remember the last time he had seen his brother this relaxed and engaged. All of his apprehension was gone and in an instant, he realized it. He quietly chuckled to himself because he didn't want to admit it. Everyone he loved was here and getting along. It was too soon, but in his heart he knew without question that this was one of the best moments of his life. For however long it lasted, he wanted to enjoy it.

"So, I gotta ask. Why do you call him Chop?" Nichelle inquired.

Slim put his beer down and began to tell Donovan's least favorite story. "When were kids. D's favorite meal was pork-chop sandwiches. Couldn't stop him from eating them. Finally, one day our pops says, 'wherever you see that boy, you gonna see a pork-chop somewhere in the area.' We been calling him that ever since."

Everyone laughed as Donovan looked at Nichelle and said, "You better not call me that."

"I would never, Pooh," she said as she kissed him on the cheek.

Donovan looked over to Rico, who had just jogged over to join the conversation.

"Where is Mama G?" Donovan asked him.

"She's in the shower. She had a long day today and said all she wanted to do was watch her soaps and sleep."

Donovan nodded, understanding that what Rico really was telling him was she didn't want to be around Slim. The two had never been as close as she and Donovan were. Still, she treated Slim like family. Donovan turned his attention back to his brother, who was examining his "Thick Nia" a little too closely for his liking.

"Slim! I'm surprised y'all not on the dominoes yet," he called out, diverting his brother's attention away from his girlfriend's thickness.

"Man, you don't want to play no bones with me! Look, when I was in the joint, me and K.T. ran the table on some bones."

Confidently, Donovan responded, "I hear you talking, but you gonna have to show me. I was born in Missouri."

"What are you talking about, Chop? You were born right here."

"Yeah, but when it comes to backing up what I say, I'm from the show me state."

The pair laughed and then embraced one another. As they embraced, Donovan whispered in his brother's ear.

"It's good to have you home."

"Yeah, we got work to do," Slim whispered in return in an unsettling way.

Donovan looked at Slim, who smiled back at him and dismissed the thought as being an over-thinker. He looked around for Nichelle, who was already making her way towards the food. He smirked because he knew she was serious about Rico's cooking. She loved it, but so did everybody else. He let her get her place in line and decided he'd go say hi to Miss Gladys, aka "Mama G," alone. When he walked into the kitchen, he saw her in the living room resting comfortably in her recliner, watching her favorite soap opera, "Days of our Lives." Donovan walked over, kissed her on the forehead, and sat next to her.

"Oh, hey baby, when you get here?" she asked. "Is your girlfriend coming in?"

"She wanted to get some food first, trying to be cute because Slim, I mean, Darrion, is here. She wanted to make a good first impression."

Miss Gladys, Rico's mother, cut her eyes as Donovan leaned back in the recliner.

"You get the money I left for you?"

"Now you know by now I'm not gonna touch any of that money. 'Cause it's –"

"Spend it or don't. It's yours to do with what you want." He said as she picked up the remote and began to poke the buttons angrily. Donovan knew she didn't approve of how they got the money. She never spent it but she never got rid of it either. He persisted on.

"So, what you watching?"

"And how long do you think Darrion is gonna be around this time?" Miss Gladys asked, ignoring Donovan's question.

Donovan got quiet. He knew he couldn't avoid this conversation.

"He's trying to change his ways."

"Now forgive an old woman, but from where I sit, that sounded like two scoops of bullshit you just tried to serve me."

Donovan smiled and nodded. Miss Gladys was like a second mother to him. In fact, she'd been his mother longer than his birth mother at this point, so there was no mincing of the words. This was his family, and she was reminding him of that.

"Mama G... It's Slim. You know he's been like this as a long as I can remember."

The woman grabbed the remote and paused her television show, brushing strands of her graying hair behind her ears as she looked at Donovan endearingly.

"Donovan, since you were nine, I knew you were a born leader. Smart kid with a good head on his shoulders. I don't worry about you much in life because I know your heart. You got good instincts and good sense."

She picked up her glass of ginger ale, took a sip, and placed it back on the table.

"Rico on the other hand, chases every waterfall he sees. He's a good person, got a good heart, but like his daddy, he trusts everybody and everyone. As I live and breathe, as much as I've done for my baby, I could never get him to learn how to use good judgment. He's real impulsive, like his daddy was. Gotta trust their guts, you know? That's what got his daddy killed. See Rico... He's loyal and doesn't realize that loyalty isn't always a two-way street. Hell, I ain't gotta tell you about Rosey. If he loves you, he'll follow you to the gates of hell. The problem is, by the time he sees it, it's too late."

"I know, Mama G. Rosey has always been optimistic. It's how we met."

Mama G turned her body to Donovan and then went deep into thought.

"That night you came to live with us. I knew you were never gonna be the same. Nobody, especially a boy, should have to see what you did and go through that. I prayed every day and night you wouldn't just lose your mind in my home because you wouldn't even talk about it, and I didn't blame you. You didn't eat for a week, and I didn't blame you for that either. But I knew if you didn't at least try to show some signs of life, we might as well have put you in the cemetery with your parents. Now I could cook, I knew that, but ain't nothing like a mama's cooking for her baby. You knew that first night you moved in what it took me an entire week to figure out. You'd never have your mama's food again, so I didn't know what to do. I thought, maybe this was a mistake. I had my baby to look after, and he was already a handful. Maybe I should call CPS. Well, the day I figured that out I realized Rico was losing weight. I never had leftovers because we both know that boy could put away some food."

"I still don't know where he puts it."

"Honey, me either, and for the first time in his young life, I had leftovers. I looked at my baby and he'd lost about 10 pounds right before my eyes. Now you know Rosey, once he makes his mind up, ain't nothing changing it. So that night, I'm at the table. I got my world-famous oxtails cooking."

"Oh, man, Mama G. Just thinking about them makin' me hungry right now."

"Oh, chile, hush. Soon as I knew you were comin', I put some in the fridge for you."

Donovan hopped up, walked over to the refrigerator, opened it, and took out one bowl to eat, saving the other bowl for Nichelle.

Miss Gladys continued, "But even with all that goodness sitting on your plate, you didn't want to eat, and I understood. But with my Rosey, I needed him to eat right then, so not really being sure what to do, I say, as quietly as possible, 'Baby, you need to eat your food.' My son picks up the fork for dramatic flair and then places it down, easy, but loud enough to let me know a fork was on the table. I turn around, and Rosey is looking me square in my eyes, and he says…"

"The next time he eats is the next time I eat," Donovan said, cutting Miss Gladys off.

She smiled and nodded her head, reliving the memory. After a spell, she looked at Donovan. "I've never seen Rosey more serious 'bout anything or anyone in this world than he was that day."

"Yeah, and every time I'd asked him, he'd say, 'I'm fine.' Finally, I just ate something so he wouldn't pass out."

"And I'm glad you did. That's when I knew that no matter how hard things were, no matter what you were going through, you were going to look after my son. And I'm so thankful for that," Miss Gladys said with a smile on her face. Her face soured and she turned her soaps back on. "Darrion has been on a path of self-destruction ever since I've known him. And to be honest, after what he's been through, I don't blame him. Now, I know that's your brother, but so is Rico, and he is my son like you're my son, and I'm asking you, please do what you can to keep my son safe because I couldn't take it if—"

"Mama G, don't work yourself up. You don't have nothing to worry about."

"Boy, tell the truth and shame the devil. I might not look like it, but I was raised on these streets. I've lived here my whole life. The same streets as you. I know the players. I know what goes on here. I know it better than all of you, which is why I want to leave one day. If you had any sense, you'd take that pretty girlfriend of yours and move far away from here and open a car wash or something and have a bunch of children. Now, I need you to promise me that no matter what you do, you'll do all you can to keep Rosey out of any serious trouble."

Donovan nodded and walked over to his surrogate mother to look her in the eyes. "I'll do whatever needs to be done to make sure Rico is safe, Mama G. You got my word."

"That's all I needed," she said with a smile.

He leaned over in the chair to hug her and decided it was time to get back outside.

"Join your friends, baby. I'm gonna finish my soaps. Just remember what we talked about."

"Yes ma'am," he replied before he headed back outside. He scanned the party for Nichelle, but it had become more crowded since he had left, and he was having a hard time finding her. He finally located Amanda, Nichelle's friend, who was back on again with Rico and walked over to her.

"What's up, Amanda? Where's Babygirl?"

"She left."

Her defensive tone caught Donovan by surprise. Something seemed off.

"Without speaking to Miss Gladys?" he responded intrusively.

Amanda fidgeted. He wasn't sure what was wrong, but he knew something had to be.

"Amanda, what's wrong?"

After a brief spell, she finally responded, "Nichelle is in trouble."

11
LAST OF A DYING BREED

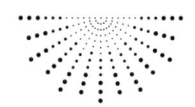

"What are you talking about? She's in trouble?"
"I wasn't supposed to say nothing, but…," Amanda paused, but Donovan wasn't in the mood for it.

"Not in the mood for games, Amanda."

"Nichelle told me she ran into Bryan yesterday in the mall. She thinks he's been following her all day and she left because she knew if you found out, you'd probably kill him. So, she left."

"Of all the stupid… Where is she now?"

"I don't know. She's just driving around trying to figure out what to do."

"Call her."

"Ok, I just…"

"Amanda, call her. Now."

Amanda dialed the number.

Donovan took the phone as Nichelle picked up.

"Girl, he's still following me. I don't know what I'm gonna do."

"This ain't Amanda."

"D… I…"

"We'll talk later. Be at my house in 15 minutes. I'll handle it."

"Donovan, I don't want you to get in any troub—"

"There you go, trying to have discussions with people that have made decisions. I said to be there in 15 minutes, and I will handle it. "

"O...k then."

Donovan hung up the phone and gave it back to Amanda. At this point, Rico was walking up.

"Yo, D? You good?"

"Yeah, man... Nichelle's ex has been stalking her for the last couple of days."

"Seriously? How do you want to deal with this?"

"I don't know, but I'm 'bout to go handle it now."

"I'm comin' too," Slim chimed in.

Donovan looked at his brother. "Slim, this party's for you. I got this."

"Chop. The strength of the wolf is the strength of the pack. You mess with one of us, you gonna see all of us. In fact, since I'm thinking about it, if your lady is going to the house, he's definitely gonna follow her. Let's run a show and tell, remember that?"

"Yeah. We're gonna show him what he's looking for and then let him tell us where he ends up by following him." Donovan said. Slim whistled in Trouble's direction, who promptly came over.

"Rico, Chop, get to your house and let it be known you see him, and once he leaves, we'll follow him away from your spot and watch my boy K.T. work cause once we put him behind the wheel, he'll never see us coming. We'll see where he ends up and have a talk there," Slim barked.

Before Donovan could respond, Slim, K.T., and Trouble were already loading in one car, which left Rico and Donovan to play their part in Slim's plan.

"Fuck it. Let's go," he said to Rico reluctantly as they headed for the car.

Once Slim got involved, he was certain things wouldn't end well, but he didn't give a fuck about Bryan. Babygirl's safety was his priority. Donovan had already taught Babygirl the main roads to get back from Miss Gladys' house because it was safer, but he knew every back road in Houston. Beating her to the house would be a minor task. He tossed the keys to Rico to drive since Donovan had to be a decoy for Bryan once they arrived. As they drove, he could feel Rico's urge to talk about Slim's uninvited involvement.

"You gotta admit, it's a good plan," Rico said, trying to be positive.

"I don't have a problem with the plan. The problem is, we're bringing a sledgehammer to squash an ant. Slim only knows one speed, and that's overkill."

"Well, it won't come to that this time, hermano," Rico said, still being upbeat.

Donovan lit a cigarette, and after a couple of puffs, he responded, "Rosey, I love your optimism, but even you gotta ask yourself when hasn't it come to that with Slim?"

The rest of the ride was silent. Donovan was partly upset at Nichelle for just not telling him what had happened. He wanted to keep his word, but this was about to get very far out of his hands. When they pulled up in front of his house, he scanned the area. He saw Nichelle's car and a car he didn't recognize across the street.

"That's gotta be him... All right, let me go rattle his cage."

Donovan got out of the car and walked across the street to the front of Nichelle's car. He stood by the door as she let the window down.

"You ok?"

"Yeah, I'm fine... Don't hurt him, please." Donovan turned his nose up at her words. She fidgeted and looked away. He took a sigh and replied.

"Not me you gotta worry about. Go inside. I'll see you soon."

He opened her car door and helped her out of the car, watching as she walked inside. All the while, he had his eye on the silver sedan. He glanced back and saw her open a curtain and give him a thumbs-up sign. Once he knew she was safe, he scanned for the sedan. Once he located it, he began walking towards the car. Confronting Bryan in his own neighborhood would cause too much attention especially being this upset. But scaring him would be easy.

"Let's try it your way, Slim," he said to himself. He pulled out his pistol and walked towards the car, which darted off quickly. He stood in the street and waited for Rico to arrive. When the black SUV pulled up, he got into the passenger seat.

"Trouble says K.T. is right on him. We'll wait for a text." Rico said.

"Cool." Donovan replied putting up his pistol.

They drove toward where the vehicle was last headed. After some time passed, Donovan wondered if K.T. was worth all the hype his brother had been bragging about.

"You think Bryan lost him?"

"Slim says this guy K.T. can drive. I'm thinking Bryan is being cautious since he knows you know what he's been up to."

"Not a big fan of this K.T. cat, if I'm being honest."

"I hate to break it to you, hermano, but you're not a big fan of anybody."

Donovan scoffed at the notion, only admitting to himself partially that what Rico said might be true. Still, there was nothing wrong with being cautious. It was a trait Rico needed more of. After a spell, they received the text.

"He's at Slick Willie's pool hall. Roughly about 15 minutes from where we are," Rico said.

"Cool."

The pair proceeded to the parking lot of the pool hall. When they arrived, Slim and Trouble were outside, leaving Donovan to ask the obvious.

"Where is K.T.?"

"He's in the car in case we need to break out quick."

"And why would we need to break out quick, Slim? We're just talking to the man, right?"

Slim smiled and walked in the door, ignoring Donovan's pointed question.

From the moment they walked into the building, a chill rushed over Donovan. As much as it annoyed him, Bryan was still around. He knew Slim was always ready for action. Donovan would've handled this with imminent discretion, but once Slim caught wind of it, there wasn't much else to be said. He was the leader of their crew. Slim enjoyed confrontation and looked for it anywhere. When he couldn't find it, he'd create it. Both of them could be ruthless, but Slim was more of a sledgehammer. It was the reason Slim had stayed in prison the full sentence time, and he had a good chance of going back.

To make matters worse, the pool hall was in a neighborhood that their crew had a reputation in. The 713 Boyz were well known in the underground of Houston. This was obvious by the way the owner looked at them once they walked in.

Donovan, aware of how this could go, turned to the owner. "You know who we are?"

"I do," the owner said nervously.

"So, what will you see?"

"Nothing at all."

Donovan took five thousand dollars out of his pocket in a band and tossed it to the owner.

"For any damages."

He diverted his attention back to Slim, who was just circling Bryan at a nearby pool table.

"Yo, Bryan? Is that you? Stalker Bryan?"

Rico and Trouble stood by the door as Bryan made moves to leave.

Donovan knew this was not going to end well. He looked at Bryan, who looked like he had aged since the last time he'd seen him. Donovan suspected he'd had a rough go of things in the past year.

Bryan turned to Slim and said, "Look, I don't know what you heard, but I don't want any trouble."

"Nobody ever wants any trouble, Bryan, but that's not how trouble works. It just shows up. That's why it's trouble," Slim said as he moved closer to the man.

Donovan examined Bryan's bloodshot red eyes. He'd been drinking and was clearly disheveled. His body looked at least twenty pounds lighter than the last time he'd seen him. A part of him regretted this moment instantly. As Slim hovered over the man, he finally spoke.

"So, you're the guy that's been stalking Nichelle... Don't take this the wrong way, but you look like a bitch."

"I ain't no bitch," Bryan said defensively.

The aggression caught Slim's attention like a wolf hearing movement from his prey nearby.

"Oh... Yeah... There's a monster inside of you, alright. One who likes to stalk women. I bet you sniff panties and other weird shit, too, don't you? I wanna talk to the monster, Bryan."

Bryan, realizing they heavily outnumbered him, composed himself.

"You got it wrong. I haven't stalked no one. I just wanted to talk to Nichelle... to apologize for the way things went a while ago."

Slim walked up face to face with Bryan, closing his fist for emphasis.

"You calling me a liar, Bryan? 'Cause I don't think that's it. I think you like scaring females. Don't you, Bryan?"

Bryan stepped back and started to rationally respond to the growing tension.

"Man, I wouldn't do that. You got it wrong. I just wanted to apologize. Drinking kinda got me in a bad way, and I wanted to let her know she was right to leave. I wasn't trying to stalk her, I swear."

Slim ignored the response altogether and looked at Donovan.

"D? I gotta tell you, man, I'm a little disappointed this is the guy that got your lady hiding. But maybe I'm just a street dude because I'd have been whipping your ass the moment you tried that shit with me. Don't you think so, Bryan?"

Donovan cut his eyes at Slim. His growing apprehension about things was about to get drastically worse.

Slim continued, "Bryan, can I call you B? I'm gonna call you B. I met Nichelle today. And meaning no disrespect, but damn she was fine. Ooh wee! She keeps it tight too."

Slim walked over and put his hand on Bryan's shoulder, who was motionless.

"You used to hit that, B? How'd you fuck that up?"

"Look, I'm not bothering anyone."

"I heard you the first time, B, but tell me something. I know it's gotta piss you off to know that she's just giving him all that ass every night. Look at him. He's probably gonna go get some pussy when we leave here. That used to be you, Bryan."

"I'll kill you, damn it!" Bryan yelled.

Donovan saw the dull rage in Bryan's eyes that he had seen the first time he met the guy.

Bryan picked up a pool stick and swung it as hard as he could, breaking it against the side of Slim's head.

Slim, un-phased by the blow, turned and looked at Bryan.

"Damn, B... You just assaulted me. But it's all good... because this is the monster I came to talk to. Let's dance."

Before anyone could react, Slim grabbed Bryan by his shirt and head-butted him viciously three times in a row with a bone-crushing force, breaking his nose and forcing him to crumble. He promptly knelt over him and began hitting him repeatedly in his face.

As blood gushed from Bryan's face, Donovan looked at the owner, who was getting squeamish. He looked over at Slim.

"Only so much blood an owner gonna be able to say was bouncer work to the cops, Slim."

Conceding his point, Slim stood up and looked down at Bryan, who was a shivering bloody pile of bones. Slim pulled out his penis and urinated on Bryan, who was too badly beaten to move.

"I know you're pissed off, B, but it's better to be pissed off than pissed on, don't you think? I think so."

"That's enough, Slim!" Donovan barked.

Slim put his package away and grabbed a pitcher of beer, pouring it on Bryan, adding insult to injury.

"Now, that's enough," Slim said, looking defiantly at his brother. He then turned back to Bryan, who was losing consciousness. "Don't be a stranger, B," he said as he walked out the door.

12
BANGING SCREW

Donovan, Rico, and Trouble stood watching Bryan bleed. He'd need to go to the hospital and honestly, he'd need to get there pretty quickly. Donovan picked up the phone and handed it to the owner.

"Call the ambulance. Tell them you were in the back and didn't see when he came in or what happened."

Donovan pulled another five grand out of his pocket and tossed it to the owner, who nodded in agreement. Even if Bryan did talk, no one wanted to be on the receiving end of what had just happened.

Despite sending a message all too clear to Bryan, Slim's deeper message was something Donovan knew had been brewing from the moment he'd gotten out of jail. The 713 Boyz were Slim's crew. Hunt or be hunted was their mindset. He didn't believe in anything else. Donovan knew what his brother was up to. He didn't care.

As they got in the cars and headed back to the party, Donovan thought about everything that had happened in the last year. His life was changing. He didn't want to do this forever. As the four men arrived at Mama G's, Donovan decided he'd go and tell Nichelle what had happened. He parked the car to say his goodbyes. As he hugged his brother, Slim spoke.

"Still gotta clean up your messes, huh, Chop?"

He wanted to let it go, but he couldn't.

"Same old Slim."

The statement made Slim pause in his tracks.

"Something you want to get off your chest about the same old me?"

"You goddamn right I do. The nerve of you calling that shit show cleaning up my mess."

"So, what would you have had me do, D? Shake the man's hand? Invite him to the cookout?"

"I didn't ask for or want your help with it."

"You mess with one of us. You mess with all of us. That's always been the code."

"Everything ain't gotta end in bloodshed, Slim," Donovan scoffed.

Slim walked over to his brother and barked, "Have you forgotten who we are? What we are? We're not the boy scouts, Chop. We're the 713 Boyz. If someone steps to us, they get stepped on."

"And what does that even mean anymore?"

"Well, that's a damn good question, Chop," Slim responded. He looked around at all the guys and continued his thought. "See, that's the problem I see with this crew. Ever since I've been gone, y'all been a little soft. You want to put a beat down on your woman's ex, but once we begin to actually beat him down, we've gone too far. It's that kind of inconsistent message that's got us out here looking weak. If you ask me. I think sa—"

"Well, ain't nobody asked you now, did they?" Donovan said, interrupting his brothers would be monologue.

He was torn, and he didn't know why. *Why am I fighting this battle?* he thought to himself. He looked at this brother and realized he knew why.

"Look, you can save the drama, Slim. I know what you're trying to do. You want to be head of your little boy's club again. Cool. I ain't got no problems with that, but ain't nobody around here soft. If you disagree, you're more than welcome to try to prove your point. Just know I don't buck as easy as that young boy you just jumped on, and I don't need no pool stick."

Donovan stood stone-faced ready to go to war with his brother if need be. Rico and Trouble stood between the two men, unsure of what was going to happen next.

Slim smiled. "Nah, all good, Chop. I just got caught up in the moment. We good," Slim said, half convincingly. He walked into the center of the men and continued, "The strength of the pack is only as strong as the wolf, so ain't gonna be no infighting between us. Besides, we have bigger fish to fry. Everyone, come by the house tomorrow morning. I got something for us to sink our teeth into, and it's major."

Donovan ignored the statement and walked to the car. Slim was the least of his concerns. Nichelle would have something to say about what happened, and he needed to deal with that sooner than later. As he drove, he thought about why she would be so concerned about a man who had abused her in the past but then dismissed the thought. When he got home, Nichelle was waiting at the door.

"Baby... Are you ok?"

"I'm good," he said gruffly.

There were no more words. Tension congested the room to the point of caution. The unspoken truth was staring at both of them, waiting for one of them to acknowledge it.

It won't be me, he decided. Donovan walked past her into the kitchen to pour a glass of Hennessy White. He took off his shirt, exposing his solid chest sharpened by his regimen of 300 push-ups a day. Walking to the bedroom, sipping the liquor, he turned on the television to watch Colombo.

Roughly thirty minutes later, Nichelle peered into the room. He didn't make eye contact and continued to watch the detective solve the murder of a judge. She walked over and sat down gingerly next to him on the bed. He glanced over and noticed she positioned her ass intentionally in view of his peripheral vision. Unbothered by her presence, he continued to watch his show. There was no question, she knew that he was furious. Nichelle slid a little closer.

"So... are... you... mad at me?" she asked.

"What do you think, Chelle?" Donovan responded, never removing his eyes from the television.

"Well... I think you're mad at me because you only call me 'Chelle' when you're mad at me, and I know you only watch Columbo when you're being spiteful since I made the mistake of getting in on one of your silly little arguments with Rico and said Monk was better than Columbo."

"Well, then, I guess you got your answer."

"Donovan, don't be like tha—"

"Why didn't you tell me about Bryan?" He barked at Nichelle who winced at his words.

"Baby, calm down you ain't gotta yell at me."

"I'm not yelling I'm—"

"Use your inside voice then," she replied sarcastically.

"I'm trying to use my inside voice but there's a lot of outside shit going on. Now tell me, why didn't you tell me about Bryan?"

She paused and looked away, then looked back at him. Finding her truth, she said,

"Yesterday I was at the mall, and I heard my name. I turn around, and I swear I didn't recognize him... he looked bad... real bad. He wreaked of alcohol. I felt sorry for him... I mean, here he was telling this elaborate lie about being on an NFL practice squad and forgot to take the name tag off of his shirt from his security job. He asked me if I had graduated, and I said yes. Then, he told me he'd left his wallet with his agent and was hungry. I felt so bad for him, so I gave him a few bucks. I thought it was just a random encounter he'd be too drunk to even remember, but when I was at the cookout, I got a text message from a number I didn't recognize. The message was, 'This is never over.' I knew it was him because he'd said that to me the last time I saw him. So, I got in the car and left and I called Amanda 'cause I didn't know what else to do."

"Cause Amanda's gonna fix it, right? How was she gonna protect you?"

"I don't need anybody's protection, Donovan. I can fight my own battles. I give you this version of me because I trust you."

"And how in the hell am I supposed to trust you, Chelle? You think your little stunt today inspired trust?"

"Do you think yours did? You say you live by a code. Well, what happened to our code, huh? When you give me your word that something is or isn't going to happen, I expect you to keep it."

"Chelle, you gotta be out of your goddamn mind if you think I was gonna stop my brother from beating the ass of my girl's ex-man because he was stalking her. And none of this would have happened if you hadn't decided to keep your dirty little secret."

"You want to tell me about secrets?" Nichelle said as her voice began to raise in frustration. "Donovan, I don't even know what you do for a living! And I know I said as long as it wasn't drugs, I was fine with it, but I'm so not fine with what happened to Bryan. Is that what you do? You go around beating people up?

"Do you want a pretty lie or the ugly truth, 'cause we can have that conversation anytime, Babygirl."

Nichelle glanced away. "You know what? A part of me doesn't want to know, but that time is coming to a close real fast. I know we agreed to just have fun, but you know it's deeper than that. I need something real, a piece of you that's real. Look, I know you're into some street shit, and if I'm being honest, maybe it's best I don't know. The thing I'm trying to say is... I'm here for you, but I gotta know that there's something to be here for. I'm asking for a piece of you... the real you."

He tried to look away, but she wouldn't let him. Her eyes invited him into a sanctuary of honesty.

"I don't want... I don't want you to judge me. None of us... I don't want you to judge none of us."

"And what makes you think I would do that?"

"Because it's been my experience that people who have, judge people who have not, and I'm a motherfucking have not."

Nichelle walked into his bulging arms, placing them around her hips, and looked into his dark brown eyes.

"Baby, you've never been a have not. You're a get up and go get. That's what I love about you, and if you can't respect that, then I don't know what you can respect… Baby, I'm not asking for any one thing. I just want to share something that is yours. Something real because I want to belong in your world."

He was quiet. He didn't know how to respond. His silence was met with disappointment, and then resolve.

Nichelle looked into his eyes again. "I'll go first. No one has ever protected me the way you have. I know that I'm strong enough to handle it, but when I tell you as a black woman how completely blissful it is to feel safe, you'll never understand. You give me that, and I thank you for it. That is my something real. I'm your Babygirl, and I'll always love you."

The words hit him. Ever since his brother was released, he knew he was bothered and he knew that Bryan was on the end of a beating that he had nothing to do with. Donovan took a sip of his Hennessy and began to tell Nichelle the hardest thing he'd ever told anyone. The truth.

13
DRAPED UP N DRIPPED OUT

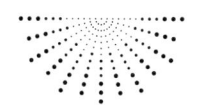

"I know what you're gonna say, and maybe some part of me doesn't want to know, but I'm not stupid, Donovan. Ever since your brother came back around, you've been off. One minute you're glad he's around, the next, you're growling. And I understand complex family relationships, but what I don't understand is why we are on this roller coaster of emotion for your brother when you just got him back."

Donovan went to sit down on the bed. He looked at Nichelle. She always seemed to have a valid point, but this time she just didn't know why he wasn't entirely ready to tell her everything. But, if there was anyone he could tell, it would be her. His Babygirl. The concern in her eyes grew, and it confirmed it was time to tell her what had been eating at him. He didn't want to address it, but she wasn't leaving him much of a choice. He lit a cigarette, and after a few puffs, he calmly extinguished it and told Nichelle everything.

"You know... Slim was more than just a brother to me. You know what I'm sayin'? We didn't really have parents... we had Clive and Maxine. They gave us birth, but... hell, even that's complicated. I don't know if I could call either of them parents, though... Maxine would always say, 'apples don't fall far from trees.' That was normally to remind us that she thought Clive was a rotten son of a bitch. When we got in trouble, she'd always say, 'What did my little rotten apple do now?' But what I always found funny was she didn't seem to realize that we fell under her tree too."

Donovan pulled out a cigarette and looked at Babygirl, who watched him with empathy. He decided he'd at least cut back on this habit and put it away again. He took a deep breath and continued.

"Maxine was right. Slim was a rotten apple, but he was my brother. And if you had your choice of Clive and Maxine or Slim to look after you, you'd choose Slim every time."

He poured himself a glass of Hennessy for this stroll down memory lane.

"When I think back, the first thing I ever remember is waking up in the middle of the night and walking into a pool of blood because Maxine had stabbed Clive in the ribcage over a game of spades."

"Wait, what? Are you seri—"

"Hey, if this is too much for you, let me know now because I don't even wanna be talking about this shit. You asked for the ugly truth, so here it is."

"You're right... it... just caught me off guard. Continue."

"Clive probably deserved it. He drank too much, and he gambled even more, which means we didn't have money, and he'd hear Maxine's mouth about that, and that was our cycle. If you're growing up and that's all you see from the age of five, it's just becomes normal to you at some point."

Nichelle sat next to him as he sipped his glass of Hennessy White while he continued.

"Maxine was a rock head. She would get high and be gone for days. Which would piss Clive off because he knew somebody had to watch the kids. It all came to a head one day. Maxine was on one of her trips but was agitated because I guess the dope was stepped on... which means it was diluted, so she was snapping at everyone. Clive told her she couldn't leave, that someone had to be here to watch the kids. Long story short, Maxine loses it, and in a moment none of us will ever forget, she tells Clive that Slim isn't even his kid. Something I think Clive had suspected all along because he'd always treated Slim like a human punching bag anyway."

Donovan finished his glass of Hennessy and poured himself another. He was fighting through his emotions for the truth. A truth he had never said aloud, the tale of his childhood. He sipped the second drink and continued.

"So, uh... Maxine goes in on this rotten apple thing, and how none of us are worth shit, and that Clive is the biggest fool of all because Slim ain't even his baby. Clive was already on a pint of tequila when she said that, but he got real quiet and sobered up real quick. He stood up and walked over to Maxine and asked, 'What did you just say?'"

Donovan poured himself another shot of whiskey and downed it. His eyes looked off into the distance as if he were somewhere else as he continued.

"She looked at him and said, 'For the last 13 years we've all been living this pretty lie, but the ugly truth is, Slim ain't even your kid. Hell, I don't know if Donovan is either.'

I've never seen Clive so calm. He got up, walked directly over to the love seat Maxine was sitting on, placed both his hands on her shoulders, and then moved them up to her neck and started choking her."

A tear rolled from his eye as Nichelle rubbed his back in a comforting and supportive manner.

"I tried to get him off of her, but he punched me right in the face. He didn't knock me out, but I wasn't able to move either. I was lying on the ground, trying to figure out what the hell had just happened to me. Maxine was smiling the whole time, so he stopped choking her and started punching her in the face as hard as I've ever seen a person hit. I screamed for help and Slim comes into the living room. He ran over and tried to get Clive off of Maxine, and Clive hit him so hard he broke three of his teeth. All the while, Maxine was laughing her face off even though it's all pummeled. Clive turns back around and starts hitting her again, and she started singing 'you can't break me,' taunting him.

Wham. He'd hit her.

'You can't break me.'

Wham. He'd hit her again.

'You can't break me.'"

Donovan grimaced before continuing, "I was eleven, and Slim was thirteen. We were doing everything we could to get Clive off of her. And all I remember thinking was, the house is so loud. Maxine was gagging on her own blood, still singing. I'm thinking she's gonna die if he hits her one more time. But then, almost like God heard my prayer, I heard a loud 'bang!' And Clive stopped hitting Maxine. In fact, he stopped doing anything. He turned to me and looked at me as if he knew something was wrong but didn't know what, but when he saw the look on my face, he knew. He looked down, and half of his skull was lying on the ground. Slim had stopped Clive. He'd gotten the gun that was underneath their mattress and shot Clive with it. I still remember how he looked at me. Like he was at peace before his eyes rolled up into the back of his head, and he fell to the ground."

Donovan took another sip of his drink and continued, "Maxine stopped laughing then. She screamed at Slim and asked what he'd done. I mean, she can't move, and she's mad at us for trying to save her life. Blood is everywhere. I'm trying to get up to find a phone to call 911. She stopped me and said, 'I'm finally free of you worthless rotten apples.' Then, she was just... gone."

Donovan rested his head between his knees as Nichelle rubbed his back. He pulled away from her to show he was fine.

"I'm ok... It's just, there's certain things a child should never see or hear, you know? That night I lost Clive, Maxine, and Slim. They didn't charge him with shooting Clive, but he was the suspect in several other cases they had opened. I moved in with Miss Gladys and Rico, but Slim was never right after that. He started using cocaine not too long after his fourteenth birthday, and he's been in and out of prison for the last fifteen years."

"I... I didn't know."

"You know what sticks with me about that day?"

"What, baby?"

"Maxine was dying. She knew it, and she could've said anything. She could've said 'I love you,' but to look at us and say that with her dying breath... it was like she wanted us to know that was all we could ever hope to be."

Nichelle took the glass from his hand and straddled him, looking him in the eyes.

"Listen to me. You are a good man, Donovan. Doesn't nobody else see you? I see you, and as long as I live, you will always have family. And I mean that, no matter what happens. If I have it, you have it. You're my rock, and we are gonna build this, whatever this is. We're gonna build us. And there will always be an us, no matter what."

Her honesty settled his war-torn soul. For the first time in his life, he felt the power of a nurturing woman. It was the first time he'd ever felt safe.

14
ASTROWORLD

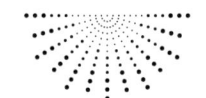

The next morning Donovan reluctantly headed over to his childhood home, where Slim was staying. When he walked into the garage, he glanced at the front door, thinking about the story he'd told Nichelle. He hadn't thought about it in years but realized he had never walked back through the front door since that eventful night. Slim was hovering, talking to the wolves, when he stopped to greet his brother.

"Glad you could make it, Chop. I was just going to tell them about Wonder Bread."

Donovan narrowed his eyes at his brother and shook his head.

"What are you cooking up now, Slim?"

Slim walked into the center of the garage. "Wonder Bread is the goose that laid the golden egg."

Donovan could tell Slim was enjoying the suspense caused by what he said. He was about to turn around and walk out when he noticed Rico also seemed to be enjoying it.

"Quit bullshitting, Slim, and tell us already," Rico said, confirming Donovan's suspicion. He wanted to leave, but now he had to stay.

"Ok, check it. When K.T. left the joint, I got a new cellmate. Palest skinned white boy you're ever gonna meet. He worked at a bank, and he was in line for a promotion, but instead of giving him the job, they gave it to this other guy. So one day, he snaps and tries to kill his boss. As he's telling me this, I'm looking at him like you're looking at me right now. I mean, who gives a shit, right?"

The other men chuckled as Slim continued.

"Except he would not shut the fuck up about it. He's my celly, so I had one of two choices. Beat the shit out of him and get some time added to my own sentence or just shut the fuck up and listen... and when you're counting down the days, having a chatterbox around passes the time. You feel me? So, I pay attention to what he's saying, and he tells me how he worked for Wilmington International Bank, who opened their flagship branch over by the baseball stadium. He was supposed to be the branch manager because he had done all the work just to get them functional and running there. Meanwhile, the guy who they gave the job to is a pill-popping peddler of prostitutes, those are Wonder Bread's words, not mine," Slim said, holding his hands in the air as if to say don't kill the messenger.

The crew laughed at the gesture, but it did not impress Donovan. He looked at Rico, who was hanging on to every word.

Don't fall for this shit Rosey, he thought to himself. He turned his attention back to Slim, who continued to build his story.

"So, Wonder Bread tells me how he'd been sending emails for months about the faulty cameras that hadn't come back online since the power outage right after the last big storm. That he doesn't feel safe because the security guard gets high every day in front of the camera and is half passed out. And, how all the systems fail when the baseball game or basketball game is happening, because the bank shares the same power grid as both of the stadiums. The most important thing he told me was this; every Thursday at 10 am, they receive 2.5 million dollars in bills that can't even be put into the vault until 3 pm because the manager is out getting his dick wet. Suddenly, it hit me. This guy is just venting, but all the while, I'm learning everything about this bank. He's literally teaching me everything I need to know in order to rob it, and that's I then started looking at him the way you're looking at me right now."

The men all exchanged fist bumps and murmurs all excited about the tale they'd just been told. Donovan still a skeptic decided to press further.

"How do you know this is true?" Donovan asked, unconvinced by his brother's testimony. Slim cut his eyes at his brother and responded.

"Uh, this might come as news to you, Chop, because I'll admit you know how to put a score together, but I was doing this thing we do while you were still playing with Power Rangers." He looked Donovan up and down, causing Donovan to roll his eyes as his brother continued to eye him.

"Damn, man, can y'all chill and act like brothers for like five minutes? At least till we get his plan," Rico said, defusing what was becoming a tense situation.

In mutual agreement they nodded, and Slim continued.

"For the last three weeks, every single day since I've been out, I've been watching the comings and goings of the good people at Wilmington International Bank. I go at different times. I sometimes set up in different locations to get different angles, and it's just like Wonder Bread said. Hell, it's worse even. The cameras don't work. When the Astros have a game, not only does the bank lose main power, but everything not on the bank's backup generator is dead, including the gate that operates the employee entrance. In fact, on those days, they just leave the gate open for a repair crew to come and work on restoring power. When the Astros or Rockets are playing, all the cops have their hands full because they are running traffic and making sure the games don't have any issues.

In two weeks, we will find ourselves in the unique position of the Houston Rockets having a home game on the same day the Houston Astros have a doubleheader. And that day is Thursday. Do you see where I'm going with this?"

"So, you're thinking we pay them a visit and take that 2.5 million dollars off their hands, and we all become half a million dollars richer," Slim's former cellmate, K.T., chimed in.

Slim pointed at him as if to confirm the answer, "You damn right."

"Hell yeah. That's what I'm talking about," Trouble said with enthusiasm.

Donovan watched as all the men expressed their excitement about Slim's plan. He looked at Rico, who clearly didn't know what he was getting himself into, and remembered his promise to Mama G.

"Yeah, that sounds good and all but me and Rosey ain't with that."

Slim chuckled at Donovan's response. "So, this is your play, Chop? You not calling the shots no more, so you're out?"

"Not in the least. I'm just not trying to go to jail."

"What are you talking about? This is a foolproof plan," Slim scoffingly replied.

Donovan shook his head and then began to break down the weak areas of the plan as only he could. Starting with the elephant in the room.

"For starters, I don't even know your boy K.T. over there, but the way he was hiding in the car when you jumped all over Bryan, I figure he'll melt if it gets hot one second."

"What did you say about me?" K.T. made his way over to Donovan, who saw through his false bravado. Donovan stood his ground, unbothered, causing K.T. to hesitate in his anger. Donovan looked at his brother.

"You see what I'm talking about, Slim? This one here is all bark and no bite."

"Fool, I should rock you right where you stand," K.T. retorted.

"Ain't nothing but air and opportunity around here, partna, so what's stopping you? Oh, that's right, you don't want to get your ass whipped up and down this garage for the next hour," Donovan said coldly. His gaze turning to steel as he saw through K.T.'s false rugged exterior into the truth of the man. K.T. had been pretending to be hard for so long it was the only character he knew how to play. The difference was, Donovan didn't have to pretend, and they both knew it.

K.T. walked away. "You lucky you're Slim's brother."

"Please don't let that stop you... I'll tell you what. Let me make it easy, K.T. If you say another word while I'm here, I'm gonna fuck you up. See, that's a threat now, so you can respond how you feel," Donovan said bluntly.

K.T. cut his eyes at Donovan, but the point was clear. He wouldn't say another word.

Slim looked at his former cellmate disappointedly and then back at Donovan.

"K.T. is the best wheel man in the game. He's gonna be behind the wheel on this. And it's a simple move, really. We get five hardhats and worker vests, some shades, and a power company van. The moment the power goes out, we show up. Walk in the back door using the manager's keycard because he'll be passed out from getting high and fucking. And then, we take it all. If anyone calls the cops they won't be able to get there before we disappear."

All the men clamored and resumed giving each other fist bumps and handshakes.

Donovan was still unconvinced. Slim was right. He had taught him everything he knew, and the plan sounded solid, but he had his reservations. And he knew anytime he had reservations to trust his gut.

"Well, good luck with that because me and Rosey ain't gonna risk our liv—"

"Speak for yourself, hermano," Rico interjected.

The words caught Donovan off guard. He stepped closer to his best friend and put his hand on his shoulder. In a low tone, he said, "Rico, if we get caught, this is federal time. You sure you want to do this?"

"I know the risk, D, but that's worth half a million dollars. Hell, I could get mom a new house and start comedy by next month."

"Rosey, you're not seeing this clearl—"

"You're my brother, Donovan, but we aren't a packaged deal. You don't have to take this gig, and I respect that, but you don't speak for me. My tongue works fine."

Donovan conceded his friend's point. *Fuck this. Why am I here?* he thought to himself. It was his first moment of genuine doubt. He thought about his night with Nichelle and realized that since she had entered his world, he had been feeling like he wanted out of the life. It was not possible for him to honor his word to Miss Gladys if Rico was there, though. He had made a promise to her because he knew what it was like to lose everything, and that was exactly what she'd be losing if something happened to Rico. She was the only person who had been there for him after his parents died. He had to be there, if not for Rico, then for her. As Slim went over the plan in more detail, Donovan chimed in.

"So, it sounds like you got everything covered except for one thing. How are you gonna get the badge to the back door off the manager?"

Slim looked up, surprised by at his brother's remarks.

"Well, right now, my plan was to get Rico to spread the word to the girls that there's an extra grand on the table to keep him occupied."

"And what about getting the badge back to him?"

"Why would we need to do that?"

"Cops come asking and find out the manager's badge is missing, they're gonna want to know where he was. You don't want them pulling at that thread."

Slim nodded in agreement and in a more welcoming tone said, "Ok, Chop. What do you think we should do?"

"I think we put Rosey on the girls, but he has to get that badge back to the manager before he wakes up. So, his job is to talk to the girls then sit at the motel until the manager passes out and when he does, Rico gets the badge, heads our way, and as soon as we get the door open, he gets it back where he found it."

Slim thought about what Donovan was proposing and nodded.

"Ok, it's settled. Rico, you're at the motel. K.T., you get the car and uniforms. Me, Chop, and Trouble are at the door. Ok, gentlemen, we know what we gotta do, so let's get it done. Let's eat."

15
MONEY MAKE THE WORLD GO ROUND

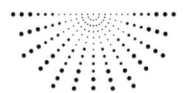

*T*he meeting was over, and everyone left except Donovan. What had begun as a whisper was growing into a roar in his head. From the moment he had committed to it, he'd felt instant regret. He had to talk to his brother alone. Slim, who was polishing a chrome Smith and Wesson .45 caliber pistol, put the weapon down and walked over to his brother, placing his hand on his shoulder.

"I'm glad we're doing this together, Chop. It's our time."

"Slim... I'm not sure I'm in on this one. In fact, I'm not sure about any of it."

Slim's eyes darkened as his frustration saturated his words. "Moth — You just said you were in. What are you talking about?"

"Since when did you start trusting outsiders? Last year you sent Carlos to us, and that didn't work out, and now K.T. Are you using again?"

"Is that what this is about? Chop, relax. Me and K.T. party from time to time, but I got my demons in check on this one. For real."

"Slim... I'm not doing this shit. If you're doped up, you're gonna get someone locked up or killed, and it ain't gonna be me."

Slim casually walked near his brother. Staring at him silently, he then asked, "You think I'm gonna get you killed? I saved your fucking life! Never forget it... You know what? Ever since you been with this Nichelle chick, I don't recognize you anymore. You went soft."

"And what about you, huh? What the fuck do you think you are?"

"I'm my own damn man. See, the thing about you running around behind this female with your nose wide open is that's exactly how Clive was with Maxine! What? Do you think she loves you? You think she's gonna be there for you? Because she won't be. The second she makes her own money, she's gonna offer to take care of you, and five seconds after that, she's gonna be on to the next dick who can afford her."

"Man, fuck you, Slim. I ain't got time for this."

"Yeah... you know I'm telling the truth. You feel that in the back of your gut, don't you? She likes them college boys, not these thugs. Is this about what happened with Bryan, or is it about something else?"

"My issue is you. Bringing in these off-brand cats to run with the 713 Boyz. We stayed out of jail for so long because we kept our circle tight."

"Have you forgotten what we are? Who we are? We're the big bad wolves. They call us that because we take what we want, when we want, from anyone we want. Drug dealers pay us just so we'll leave them alone. The streets are afraid of us. When me and Rico had to do our time for that robbery, and it was just you and T out there, I thought the streets was gonna try to come after our name. But what did you do?"

"We went back and finished the job," Donovan answered grudgingly.

"You robbed the same motherfuckers we got locked up behind. That sent the streets a message. The 713 boys are savage, and if you mess with the pack, you gotta catch or kill them all because they'll keep coming. We were born for this hunt and I'm gonna make sure we make more money than we've ever seen in our lives by growing the pack."

"But when does it stop, Slim?"

Slim looked confused at first, then he smirked. "Stop? I don't want it to stop. I want it to grow... You remember hearing stories about the Smurfs when we were growing up?"

"Everyone knows about the Smurfs. They were one of the city's most legendary gangs. What's your point?"

"You think they wanted it to stop?" Slim said as he picked up another pistol and began to polish it. He continued, "Nah, Chop. They wanted the entire city to know who they were because even in hell, someone has to be king. I want to be mentioned with the likes of the Smurfs and the Southside Hustlaz. When I'm done, we gonna be legendary. I never want them to forget the 713 Boyz."

Donovan realized there was no convincing his brother. His ambitions were larger than even this heist. The streets were all he wanted to know.

"When we were kids, we use to go up to Hobby airport and just watch the people come in off the planes. We'd guess where they were coming from, and it was all innocent. Then one day you had the bright idea to start stealing from the passengers. We did good for a few weeks but eventually we got caught. I say that because I feel that way right now. I'm not feeling this play, Slim. I'm out."

Slim smiled. "Is that how you wanna play your hand, Chop? 'Cause I'll tell you right now, you can do what you want, but as you heard, Rosey is with me, and if you think I'm gonna not put him on the front lines kicking in the door next to me, you've got another think coming. See, the only way your little plan to save your friend works, is you gotta be there to make sure it does. That's right. Don't think I didn't know what you were doing just because I let it happen. What the fuck is wrong with you? Ain't no way out of this game."

Slim started to fume as he spoke. He put the pistol down and looked his brother in the eyes. "You know what I remember about them airplanes? All those people would get off and go somewhere else but none of them ever came to help us. This country don't give a damn about us, Chop. When it comes down to it, it doesn't matter how much money you got. Guns is the only currency that matters and you're good at that. You been robbing motherfuckers since you were eight. You think you get a retirement package? We're the 713 Boyz. Hunting is what we do. Get on board, and stop being a bitch about it."

Rico's words came back to him. *We can't do this shit forever.*

He thought about the promise he'd made to his surrogate mom. Slim would land Rico right back in jail. And the only way to make sure he was as far as possible from the actual action was to be there in his place. His word was his bond. He was comfortable walking away if Rico wasn't involved and could live with his name being sullied for that betrayal. But walking away now, leaving Rico to do this job alone, wasn't something he could live with. *Half a million would be enough to finally get out. For good,* he thought to himself. Being through wasn't much of an option. In for a penny, in for a pound.

"Alright, Slim. You made your point. Let's hunt."

16
UNTOUCHABLE

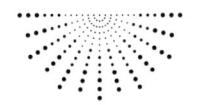

"We're almost out of time."

"Babygirl, will you relax? They promised to get back to you today."

"But what if they forgot?"

"You are tripping very hard right now. You're gonna get the—"

"Shhhh! You trying to jinx this? Hush your mouth."

Donovan laughed at Nichelle, who was pacing back and forth. She was waiting on news about her interview with Burrows Industries. The hiring manager would inform the new candidate today.

"You should've seen the company. It was so diverse. I loved it... What if they don't like me?"

Donovan put the gun down that he was oiling. He gently grabbed her by the arm and ushered her onto his lap. He looked into her eyes lovingly and responded.

"How could anyone not like you? You're smart, beautiful, and sexy. A born leader that knows when and how to follow. Trust me, you're gonna get the j—"

"Donovan. Quit playing. Don't say the word."

"What word? Oh, you mean don't say you're gonna get the j—"

"I mean it, baby," she said in a serious tone. She was nervous.

"Fine. But you're tripping. The moment they saw you, they were going to hire you because you came in, you looked the part, and you talked the part. You're overreacting."

Nichelle stood up and paced again. "You know what? You're right. I had a damn good interview. I bought the right outfit and had on the right shoes. I looked like I belonged there."

Donovan was silent for a moment. His conversation with Slim echoed in his head. He wanted to ask her about it, but wasn't sure how to bring it up.

"You know, I'm always gonna be some version of this, right?"

Nichelle looked at him. "Where did that come from?"

"I'm just saying, your life is about to change, but that's your life. My life ain't changing anytime soon."

Still looking at him blankly, she walked over to him and hugged him unexpectedly. "Donovan, I love you for you. I hope you know that. But right now, that's not important. I gotta get the job first, and I don't know if that's gonna happen."

"It's gonna happen, Babygirl, because I can't think of anyone more focused than you. You know your shit. I've never met someone more prepared or driven. They'd be foolish not to hire y—"

"Donovan. Hush. Don't say anything.... but you're right. I was prepared... yeah.... you're right," she said as she paced back and forth.

Donovan was oiling his gun for the upcoming heist, and he enjoyed the distraction because his mind was still torn about telling her at all. In all the time since they'd been together, he'd never taken a risk this big. Still, it was refreshing to hear her excited, and, more importantly, distracted.

After a few steps, she turned back to him. "But what if I don't get—"

"Nichelle if we're talking about it, then let's talk about it, but, if not, let's do something else."

"Ok, well, if you want to talk about something else, you can start with what's been eating at you lately."

Her words startled him. She may have been distracted, but she was aware. Donovan conceded her point and told her.

"It's Slim."

"Of course it is."

"What does that mean?"

"Nothing... It's just that ever since Slim has been around, it's been hard to recognize you."

Donovan chuckled. "That's funny because he said the same thing about me since I've been with you."

Nichelle rolled her eyes and took a seat next to him as he put the gun down.

"He's.... gonna put Rico in an unpleasant situation, and I promised Miss Gladys I'd keep Rico out of unpleasant situations. I know Rico is trying to do his comedy thing, and I don't want Slim to ruin that. At the same time, I'm tired, Babygirl. I'm tired of living like this. I've made every choice in my life, and it got me here. No matter what I do, I can't get ahead."

Nichelle got up and sat in her lover's lap. She kissed him on his forehead.

"Do you remember the night we met? Before my crazy ex-boyfriend or the explosion... Do you remember our first conversation?"

Donovan thought back to the night in question and grinned. "I remember. What about it?"

"I hadn't even known you for an hour, but it felt like I'd known you my whole life. The one thing that was true then, and is true now, is this: You will probably get into some trouble here or there, but your heart is in the right place. That's why I don't pressure you about what you do anymore because I know, deep down, you're doing what you feel is best. If your heart is in the right place, which I believe it to be, then I gotta trust you're making the best decisions for everyone involved. That's how I show you I love you."

Her words surprised him. Stunned by their clarity, he pulled her closer to him and kissed her on the shoulder.

She rubbed the top of his low-cut fade and ran her fingers down to his chin before continuing. "Look, I don't know Slim, but I know Rico. He's had your back since the day I met you and you've had his. I'm not sure what the issue is, but if Rico needs you, you've gotta be there for him."

"It's not that simple. Slim's gonna –"

"If something happened to Rico and you could have controlled the outcome, would you regret not doing anything?"

"Well... yeah."

"Then it's that simple. I may not like it. Miss Gladys may not like it, but that's your brother, every bit as much as Slim is. You gotta make sure he's safe because Lord knows that boy won't ever look after himself."

Donovan processed Nichelle's words. She had a way of being right, even when she was clueless. In this case, it was exactly what he needed to hear. He watched her eyes as she examined the pistol he'd been polishing, and he knew she was saying some of this for his benefit. Donovan pulled out two glasses from the cupboard where he kept his Gentleman Clive whiskey and poured a glass for him and Babygirl. After a sip, he responded.

"I don't want to look after Rico, or anyone for that matter... not forever. Sometimes I think about just leaving the city and starting over someplace else.

"Boy please, you couldn't leave Rico and Miss Gladys, and you couldn't leave Slim now that he's back."

"I'd leave for you."

Nichelle chuckled at first, but then looked back at his eyes, unwavering in their testimony. She took a sip of her drink and responded.

"You would leave for me? Do you mean that?"

"Yeah, man. I mean, we could go someplace like... L.A. or Atlanta and start over. Just me, you, and Rocky."

"I almost fell for it. Donovan, Houston is in your blood. You wouldn't make it a week before you'd be homesick. What would you even do out there?"

"Shit, I don't know... I'd... get a car wash or something like that, 'cause it never rains in California, right? So, them motherfuckers always would need their cars washed, and I can do that shit. It wouldn't take much."

Nichelle pulled out her phone. "Babe, we'd probably need like half a mill to get a car wash started in Atlanta."

Donovan took another sip of his drink and exhaled as he mulled over the number. *Split five ways that's not much more than the score Slim is talking about.*

"Babe, what are you thinking?"

"I was just thinking... That's not a lot of money when you think about it, for Atlanta... hell, that's not a lot of money at all."

She kissed him. "Hell, Houston's so big we can just move to Katy or Sugarland and be in a whole 'nother world. Especially if I get this... phone call. They have offices all over the country. We can move anywhere. I like this plan. All we need now is half a million dollars," she said jokingly.

"Yeah. That's all... we... need," Donovan responded, now incentivized by the conversation he was having with his lover. Instinctively, he picked up his pistol as he was daydreaming along with Nichelle.

She watched him.

"Stand up. We'll pass the time another way. Show me what we've been working on," he said as he ejected the clip and bullet in the chamber from the gun. He took her hand and placed the unloaded weapon in it. "This is how you hold a pistol," he said, placing the weapon firmly in her hand as he stood next to her. He examined her holding the pistol. "I want you to plant your feet first and find a natural base. You need to find a comfortable firing stance for you, so if you're handling a weapon with some actual power, you won't get knocked over."

He inspected her as she spread her feet apart, shoulder length. "Next, make sure your arms are fully extended with your dominate hand high on the handle and your trigger finger resting outside of the trigger. Your non-dominant hand is at the bottom of the gun, so you don't accidentally eject the magazine. Grip the handle tightly, but not too tight."

"Harder than I hold it when I'm giving you head?"

"Look, freak-nasty, pay attention. But yeah, a little harder than that. You want to feel like you're in control of the weapon and that it won't fly off, so have a firm grip. Finally, just take a deep breath and hold it as you aim for your target. I made sure the gun is empty so you can squeeze the trigger to get a feel for the entire motion."

She aimed at a vase that was sitting on the nightstand.

He observed her as she became familiar with the weapon. He knew the feeling she was experiencing. The one that came with holding an instrument that determined life or death. She now had the means to protect herself and ensure her own survival. She had power.

Nichelle aimed at the vase and took a deep breath as she pulled the trigger.

Click.

He nodded. Her stance was a little off, but she understood what she needed to understand. He then took the pistol, reloaded it, and handed it back to her.

"I'm giving you this gun for your own safety. You're ready now. If you ever have to pull this gun, remember to do that—"

"I gotta pull the trigger. I know, babe."

"And why is that?"

"Because if you've gotten to the point where you feel you need to pull a gun, your life is already in jeopardy," she murmured as she rolled her eyes.

Donovan nodded in agreement.

"You're actually much better than you were when we started."

"Well, I've done this every day at the drop of a dime since Bryan. I'm getting the hang of it. He's still in the hospital by the way."

"Yeah? Well, actions have consequences."

"Whatever. You can say what you want, but you didn't have to do that. Anyways, do you know what pistol I really wanna see?"

"Nichelle, this is serious, I just —"

"Your 10-inch pistol. I want your dick moving in between my legs at brutal speeds. Can you do that for me?"

She widened her eyes pleadingly.

Donovan smirked. "Well shit. We can always take a rain ch—"

Buzz. Buzz.

Their sexual banter same to an immediate halt as her phone rang. Her eyes filled with anticipation. She put the gun down and paced frantically.

"That's them. That's Burrows Industries."

Buzz. Buzz.

She held the phone in her hand and jumped up and down. "Baby, it's them. They're calling me!"

"Babygirl, if you don't answer the phone, they won't be calling you much longer."

"Oh, you're right. What should I do?"

"Answer the damn phone!" he said, slightly confused by her hysteria.

Buzz. Buzz,

She unlocked her phone and answered. "Hello? This is Nichelle."

He watched her face as it went from nervousness to excitement.

"Yes sir. Thank you, Mr. Burrows. I can't tell you how much this means to me. I won't let you down."

Nichelle hung up the phone and let out a scream. "I got the job!"

17
SIMPLY BEAUTIFUL

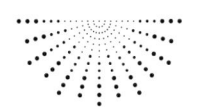

Donovan snuck out of bed while Nichelle was still asleep and cooked breakfast. Today was her first day at Burrows Industries and he wanted it to be special. He also needed to clear his mind because it was also the day he planned on getting half a million dollars richer. Today was his last robbery. He made her favorite, bacon, eggs, and vanilla-cinnamon pancakes with a side of hash browns. As the bacon cooked, he walked over to the closet and quietly pulled out three boxes and placed them on the table alongside a card.

By the time he finished the hash-browns, his mind had run over the plan in his head many times. He'd gone with his brother to case the bank and, indeed, everything he'd told them two weeks prior was exactly as it was then. He felt confident. Still, he knew this was an enormous risk. There was no room for error.

Around the time the food was done, Nichelle, awakened by the aroma, joined him. "Babe... Is this for me?"

"You know it. You got a big day today. We gonna start this thing off right," Donovan said as he walked over and kissed her on the cheek. "Go sit at the table. Breakfast is done."

"Oh, shit! You made vanilla cinnamon pancakes? I know it's special now because you never make these unless you're apologizing."

"Or unless there is a special occasion and you, shining like the star you are, are worth a little extra effort."

"You better be careful or I could get used to having this every day."

"But wait... there's more," he said, pointing to the boxes he had set out.

"Ok, I see you, big daddy. You know I like gifts," Nichelle said as he placed the food on the table and poured her a glass of ice-cold strawberry lemonade.

"Just a lil somethin' somethin'," he said.

"You trying to win the throat 'n thighs award this early in the morning?"

Donovan chuckled at the sexual innuendo and replied, "Is it working?"

"Definitely... There's a card too. Let me see what you gotta say." Nichelle opened the card and read it.

BABYGIRL,

First, let me say how proud I am of you. You're living your dream and that's not an easy thing to accomplish. I... ain't ever had nobody believe in me the way you have. Every day we spend together is a privilege for me. I have to be real and say I've seen you growing... and I don't know where I fit into the new life you're creating. I ain't perfect, and I know that being with me ain't always easy, but I hope you know this: I love you, Nichelle. I've known that since the first time we kissed... and ever since that day, everything I do has been for you. You are the reason for my thoughts and my actions. You're my Babygirl, and being with you is the dream I never thought I could have. Well, anyway, I just wanted to say congratulations and kill 'em at work today.

Donovan.

NICHELLE WIPED TEARS FROM HER EYES. "BABY, THIS IS SO THOUGHTFUL. All of it. I mean breakfast, this heartfelt note... You definitely won the throat award," she said jokingly, continuing to wipe the tears from her eyes.

Donovan, in a similar joking fashion, pumped his fist in the air as if he'd won.

Nichelle picked up the first box and looked at it curiously. "Now what's in these boxes?"

As she opened the boxes, she was speechless. Donovan, uncertain of his gifts, clarified his thought process.

"So, I need to tell you the story behind this. I figured you needed some clothes for the first day of work, so I went to that store you always be talking about in the Galleria."

"Nordstrom?"

"Yeah, that one. Well anyway, I'm in the store, right, and I figure you're in here all the time, so I talked to one of the clerks and kinda described you, and they pointed me to a lady named... Sabrina... I think it was?"

"Wait... so Sabrina helped you pick this out?"

"Yeah, I guess for the kind of bread you spend in there, they give you a personal shopper if you're a regular. Which now I know where all my damn money is going. But that's beside the point. So, I tell Sabrina let me get the same thing you had on for the interview but in a different color, and she asked 'Did she get the job?' I said, 'Yeah.' She gets up and is gone for like 30 minutes. She comes back with this business suit and some of those red bottom shoes you always talkin' about too. Then I went down to the apple store and got you the best Mac laptop they had because I know them corporate cats always have Mac computers. I didn't want you to stand out."

Looking into his eyes, Nichelle replied, "The first time I went to Nordstrom I was daydreaming about what it would be like to shop there. And nobody gave me the time of day, but Sabrina. She helped me to develop this amazing fashion sense you see before you today. We always talk about what I wanted to wear the first day of work... and this is it. Right now, at this moment, I have everything I've ever wanted, and I'm sharing it with you. You fit right here in the center of my heart. I love you, Donovan Brown, and I always will. Whatever we're building is ours and we built it together."

Nichelle stood up and walked over to Donovan, who was leaning against the hallway wall. "You know what this means, don't you?"

"I won the thighs award too?"

She wrapped her hands around his neck and kissed him gently. "You won the throat and thighs award," she said she smirked. She kissed him and rubbed his chiseled naked chest.

Donovan lifted Nichelle off of the ground into his bulging rock-hard arms and carried her into the bedroom, tossing her effortlessly on the bed as if she were a small pillow. He pushed up her purple satin nightgown far enough for her to take it off entirely.

"This is your day. You're getting breakfast' n' head."

"I like the sou—Oh my God."

Donovan buried his face into her pussy lips, calling her clitoris awake. "Good morning, beautiful," he murmured as he held her clit firmly in between his lips.

"Donovan, what are you...? Oh God, yes," she moaned in agonizing pleasure as he took several long egregious licks to her flesh before settling on a quicker precise motion in the most sensitive corner of her clit.

"Oh my God! Do not stop!" she howled.

He wouldn't until he heard the words he was working for.

"God...I'm... cum..ing," she yelled, overwhelmed by the pleasure his tongue was producing. Her body went limp.

She was still feeling the aftershocks when he pulled down his sweatpants and slid inside of her. He stroked her as she opened her legs to receive him. With each stroke from his dense cock, desire re-entered her body. She wanted more. Her pussy tightened around his dick as he dove deeper into her walls.

"Well, fuck me then," she said, fully aroused again.

He persisted in digging into her core. She was dripping wet thanks to him and was only getting wetter with each thrust. The sound of their two bodies meeting now echoed throughout the home.

She squealed at the top of her lungs with each thrust as he stroked her with a craftsman's touch. She dug her nails into his waist as he continued to punish her with pleasure. By now her legs were sitting comfortably on his broad, muscular shoulders.

He bit her right calf slightly, adding a twinge of pain to her pleasure, something she enjoyed.

Her hair unraveled, and she smiled, knowing he could feel the moisture saturating his thick solid dick and the idea that he knew turned her on even more.

"I said fuck me then!" she barked.

He picked up the pace. The more he fucked her, the wetter his cock became.

Her eyes rolled in the back of her head as she submitted to his powerful thrust. She yearned for more and he provided. "Damn it... don't... stop."

He was cumming, and he knew it. He could feel the fluid leak onto the sheet as she rolled her eyes and submitted to him, fully overwhelmed by pleasure. Her eyes confirming not only her satisfaction, but permission to do whatever he wanted with her. Her body was a willing participant in anything he did next and as bad as he wanted to release inside of her at this moment, he wanted more of her. He flipped her on her side and ran his dick deep inside her, the width of his shaft constantly rubbing against her G-spot. Her ass cheeks bounced against his thighs as he continued to stroke her. Her caramel titties excited him, bouncing in rhythm with her ass. She was going to cum again, and this time he was going to join her.

"Fuck!" he moaned savagely. He released his seed, filling her tight, wet pussy with his sweet, sticky semen. Donovan could go no further. He collapsed next to her in exhausted satisfaction.

"Just.... where in... the hell... did that come from?" she asked, panting to catch her breath.

"I just want you to know how much I'm gonna be thinking about you on this day."

As they laid there, Al Green's *Simply Beautiful* came on her playlist. She smiled.

"The first night I met you, this song was playing on the way home. This was my parents' favorite song."

"They loved them some Al Green, huh?"

"Sure did, but I fell in love with his voice too. It was the happiest time in my life when me and my brothers would listen to it, even when they weren't around. But when I hear this song now, his voice reminds me of yours."

"I don't sound like—"

"Let me finish. When I hear your voice, I feel safe... like there's nothing we can't do together. I feel... loved."

"I never want to forget this moment," he said. Her words touched him dearly. He rested his head on her bare left breast, listening to the sound of her heartbeat as she continued.

"I want many, many more moments like this with you, Donovan Brown. I want you to marry me."

"You know, I was thinking, this is the first time I've ever been this happy. Thank you. To me, you are simply beautiful."

The words and the song nestled in his chest as they sat in silence as the rest of the song played. Every note of their bodies gently bounced to a slow romantic dance of clarity between two lovers, understanding that there was something bigger than the both of them. It was happening. They were, without fail, becoming one. As the song ended, they let the silence linger for a spell to settle into their spirits.

The more he held her, the more her uneasiness fought the fog of pleasure to asked a pointed question. "Donovan. Is everything ok?"

He pondered her question. He'd never been this vulnerable before, this open. He wanted to tell her everything uncompromisingly. For a year, they had flirted around with what he did and it had worked for them, but she was growing, and he didn't want to hold her back. No. He couldn't tell her. She had never asked.

"Yeah... I'm just happy for you, that's all. I love you. Now get up, you got to get to work."

Nichelle hit him playfully on the shoulder. "Goddamn it, Donovan. Today is my first day, and I done already forgot I have a job. My hair is a mess, I can't feel my legs, and you want me to get up, shower, and be focused enough to process what, exactly? What work do you think I'm gonna get done with me like this? Fooling around with you, I'm 'bout to get fired on my first day. I need a nap. Shit, you know how to use that thing. My cookie is still pulsing. I'm supposed to be at my best today. You better not get me fired."

Donovan kissed her. "Drink some coffee. Get up. It's time for the first day of the rest of your life."

She snuggled underneath his chest and gently bit his nipple. "First day of *our* lives. You know what I was thinking is maybe once I get my check, I can start holding us down until you figure out what it is you want to do."

The words caught Donovan off guard. He looked at her hauntingly as she stood to head to the shower. "So, you plan on holding me down?"

"Look, we just had a good morning, so don't start with that toxic masculinity bullshit. Please, baby."

Donovan got out of the bed. Whatever he had been feeling was just lost at her words, something she caught on to instantly.

"Donovan... I didn't mean it like that. I was just saying we could... I mean we're a team. I got you the same way you got-"

"All due respect, Babygirl, I've been taking care of myself my whole life. I ain't never been the type to let another person take care of me."

"I meant nothing by it, baby, I'm sor—"

"It's all good. Don't sweat it. Get ready for work. You got a big day."

Donovan kissed her on the forehead and looked her in the eyes, unsure of his emotions, but certain that no matter what happened, Slim's words would echo in the chambers of his mind. Whatever uncertain feelings he had about this next job were gone. He needed the money, and was going to do whatever it took to get it. Leaning against the dresser, he watched silently as Nichelle finished her hygiene regimen and dressed for the first day of her new job.

As she turned to walk out the door, she stopped and said, "Baby, don't do nothing stupid, today."

The words startled him, catching him off guard with their directness. He wasn't sure how to respond, so he responded with the same honesty that he'd always had with her.

"Do you want a pretty lie or do you want the ugly truth?"

"Don't do that shit with me, Donovan!" she barked.

He wanted to continue to be defensive, but he could see her anger collapsing under a more vulnerable nature. She was hurt by him, and wouldn't be able to handle whatever he was doing because she was, more now than she had ever been, Nichelle Myers. She wasn't his Babygirl anymore, whether he wanted to admit it or not.

"Damn it, Nichelle. I just gave you the best morning I know how to give a woman. Ain't that enough?

"Donovan, you doing nice things is you doing nice things. But no, it's not enough. I want... I need more. I'm tired of us both pretending like you aren't into some foul shit."

Donovan scoffed at her words. He took out a cigarette and lit it. After a puff, he responded.

"Yeah, the same foul shit that's got your ass draped in luxury from head to toe."

"But that ain't—"

"I wasn't done. Now, when you met me, you had every inclination of what I was. Over the last year, I ain't really gave you no indication otherwise. I'm never wearing a suit to work. And you were cool so long as you looked good and ate good and were fucked good. Well, here we are, Babygirl. Your first day of work and you look good. You ate good, and, based on the scratches on my back, you were fucked good too. So, you want to have this conversation because you're about to get a little money in your pocket. That's cool, but don't act like you haven't been around here doing your best Ray Charles impersonation. Because with me, the ugly truth is all around you."

Nichelle stared silently.

Donovan took another puff of the cigarette and then put it out in the ashtray.

"I'm gonna be late for work. We can talk about this later."

As she turned to leave, Donovan grabbed her by her arm and looked into her eyes. "It's gonna be different soon. I promise."

"Ok... We can talk about it tonight," she said unconvincingly.

He could tell his words had hurt her. He wanted to let her know tonight he really meant that he was going to change, but there was nothing he could do about it now as she walked out the door.

18

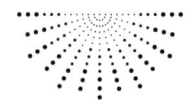

DREAMS

"You bitches ready to get rich?" Donovan said as he walked into the abandoned warehouse on the south side of town.

Trouble, Slim, and K.T. all looked up and nodded.

Rico turned around and smiled. "Hermano, you made it!" Rico said as he approached his best friend. The two men exchanged a hug.

"I couldn't let you do this by yourself, brother. Besides, what would I do when y'all boys move to River Oaks or Sugarland and I'm still in South Park?"

"I'd let you visit," Slim chimed in as he walked over and gave his brother a hug as well. Leaving his hand on Donovan's shoulder, Slim turned around and barked. "The 713 Boyz are about to put themselves on the map!" The sound of his voice bounced off the walls of the warehouse.

All the men exchanged handshakes and high fives as they settled in on the idea of becoming half a million dollars richer.

"What about Nichelle? Does she know?" Rico asked as he examined his 9-millimeter pistol.

"No need. Once I'm done with this, I'm out."

"Moving on up to the east-side to a deluxe apartment in the sky, huh?" Slim said as he walked back over to the center of the men.

"The way I see it, this is the last robbery any of us have to pull. So yeah, kinda. When is go time?"

"Rosey was just about to head out," Slim answered.

"Yeah, Slim's right. I'm gonna bounce as soon as Melinda gives me the word. She's waiting for the bank manager right now. So, once I get the text, I'll go by the motel, grab the key card, and we're in on a beach somewhere."

"Let's hope it's that easy," Slim said. He walked to the table where the ammo was sitting and continued to load his weapon. When he finished loading the pistol, he said to the group. "The first game has already begun and the Rocket's game begins in about another hour, so that's our window of opportunity."

"We gotta move quick once it's go time. Just stick to the script," Donovan chimed in.

"I still can't believe you, man. Neecie's a good girl. She might not have liked it, but she's down for you. I think you're withholding a major part of your life, bro."

"Did you tell Amanda where you are today?"

"Well, no, because we're just fucking. You're practically married with a kid if you count Rocky."

"All I want to know is, who's the bride?" Slim laughed.

Everyone, including Donovan, chuckled at his brother's ribbing.

Slim continued, "Now if you two can quit this emotional shit and focus on the task at hand, we're about to get more money than we've ever seen. Once we do that, I'll be right by your side to give you away as you walk down the aisle, but right now, focus up."

"You right, bro. My bad," Donovan responded.

Slim stopped when he was about to walk off and said, "Although I will say you got some trust issues, Chop. You gotta let your bitch into your thoughts and feelings in order to have a healthy relationship. Hoes love honesty. She looks like she can handle you keeping it a hundred."

Donovan shook his head at his brother's toxic honesty. "Slim? Do you ever hear yourself?"

"What? What did I say?"

"Nothing... So, is this the van?"

"Yeah. K.T. couldn't get a utility vehicle, but we got some company decals to slap on the van. It's gonna do just fine."

"Cool, and what about the utility outfits?"

"Sitting over there on the table next to the ammo."

Donovan put on the utility outfit. Once he was finished, he looked for the last piece. "Where's the neon vest?"

"I could only get two vests," K.T. responded.

"And let me guess, one for you, one for Slim." Donovan cut his eyes at his brother who was checking his pistol.

Never looking up, Slim responded, "Chill out, Chop. If K.T. says he couldn't get it, then that's what it is."

"Whatever man, let's just go." Donovan looked over at Rico, who was checking his burner phone.

"Melinda just said the manger is enroute, so I'm gonna bounce. I'll meet you guys at the bank."

Donovan walked with Rico towards the end of the warehouse. As Rico was about to get in the car, he said, "Look if something goes south..."

"Will you chill out? This is a full proof pl—"

"Rosey... If something goes south, promise me you'll get out of there. For me and for Mama G. She can't afford to lose anyone else."

"That's pretty dirty to bring this up right now."

"Last time you went away, it nearly killed her. Rico, promise me."

Rico tilted his eyes downward. "OK, I got you, hermano, but you worry too much and so does she." He got in his car and left.

Donovan walked back in and saw Slim checking the car.

"You give your little brother a kiss and pack his lunch for him?"

Donovan ignored his brother's comment and said, "I got ski masks and shades for all of us. We put them on soon as we get through the first gate, the silent alarm has to be on generator power, so let's assume that we only have ten minutes inside. Anything we don't get in ten minutes, we gotta leave."

Slim hit the side of the van twice and smiled. "Decals look good."

Donovan looked at the van, the first thing that hadn't gone according to the original plan, and then turned to his brother.

"So, what really happened with the utility vehicle, Slim?"

"Doesn't matter now, does it? Besides, it's more space for the money and we can rip these decals off and move around without any real problems."

"You don't think pulling up in a white van is gonna raise a red flag?"

Slim turned to his brother. "Chop... How many people you know remember what the energy company pulls up in? Zero. They just want the fucking power back on. So, we slap a Center-Point logo on it and we're good."

"I hate to break this bickering up, but we gotta bounce," Trouble said, rubbing his hands together.

Slim put his hand on Donovan's shoulder. "Relax, Chop, in a couple of hours we're all gonna be a little less on edge. Let's go, ladies, it's time to hunt!"

The crew got inside the van with K.T. in the driver's seat. The bank was about forty-five minutes away with no traffic. Donovan turned his full attention to the job at hand. Slim may have trusted K.T., but he hadn't survived this long in the game by trusting what other people thought about men. He looked them in the eyes, and from what he could see, K.T. was a coward. Still, he was in the game now. He had no choice but to follow through.

They took the back roads to the outskirts of downtown while listening to *Hail Mary* by Makaveli on repeat. After a while, they were downtown. Traffic was light, but the games were beginning. The power would be out at any moment. It was go-time.

"There's your boy," K.T. said as they pulled up next to Rico's car. As soon as he got out of the car to get in the van, Donovan knew something was the matter with his friend.

Rico got in the van and sighed, looking at the four men positioned in the back ready to take action.

"I met with Melinda. He doesn't have a key card."

"He what?"

"Apparently, he lost it a few days ago and is waiting for a new one, so, for now, he just goes through the front door."

"Son of a... Motherfucker!" Slim said he punched the back wall of the van. He rubbed his shaved head with both hands before letting his frustrations get the better of him. "You meant to tell me we got 2.5 million dollars just waiting for us on the other side of a door we can't open? Fuck!" Slim said as he punched the wall for a second time.

"Maybe we should turn around," K.T. said.

Donovan glanced over at the man, who was sweating profusely.

"We're not leaving empty-handed," Slim barked back.

"I feel you, Slim, but it just seems lik—"

"We are not leaving empty-handed. If you're not willing to put in the work to get this bread, then maybe you shouldn't eat off of it. But know this, ride or die, we're gonna get this dough."

"Man, I'm just saying, it's a lot happening wrong right now. I can't go back to jail, Slim."

Narrowing his eyes, Slim scoffed, "K.T., are you turning bitch right now? I can't believe this shi—"

"Y'all both chill," Donovan interjected. "We'll deal with that shit off the field. Right now, we gotta figure out how to get in this door. Any ideas?"

Trouble, who was often quiet, chimed in. "We could kick in the do—"

"Trouble, we can't go in guns blazing," Slim said, cutting him off. "We gotta buy ourselves as much time as possible. That means no loud noises, fool, 'cause that will definitely trigger the silent alarm and the cops will be on our ass in no time. We need the element of surprise. Besides, if we hit that door hard, we're in a shootout with security. Damn it. I can't believe this shi—"

"I can do it," Rico interjected.

Donovan looked at this best friend, knowing he was the right man for the job, but also knowing that meant he'd have to be right in the thick of things. That would make it harder to leave. He wanted to convince Rico otherwise, but looking in his eyes he knew Rico wasn't going to back down. The stakes were already high, and they were too close.

Sorry Mama G, he thought to himself. He turned back to the squad and said, "Rosey can get in that door. We're gonna be tight on time, but if that door has no primary power, Rosey can disable the lock."

Slim looked at his brother, then at Rico, and nodded.

"Soon as the power is dead, we're moving. Rosey... take K.T.'s uniform."

"What? Wait, a second. I need this uniform," K.T. chimed in. "What if the cops com—"

"For the love of God, quit acting like a bitch. Give him the goddamn uniform so we can all get this bread," Slim said in frustration.

Donovan looked at Slim, who nonverbally acknowledged he was right about K.T.'s poise.

K.T. took off the uniform for Rico, and Donovan handed Rico a ski mask and shades to accompany the uniform he had on.

Moments later, the block lost power.

Slim grinned devilishly and said, "It's time to get that bread, hunt or be hunted. Let's eat."

19
AND NIGHTMARES

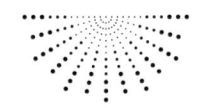

The crew waited fifteen minutes before pulling up to the gate, which was indeed open.

Donovan took a drag of his Camel cigarette and then ashed it. He clutched his 9-millimeter pistol. His breathing was rhythmic and steady, his eyes focused on anything that moved too suddenly. He was as aware as he'd ever been. The cotton in the mask he was wearing absorbed the sweat from his brow. He felt like his body was on fire, with adrenaline rapidly coursing through his veins.

Slim looked at the four men who were now going to enter the building. "Yeah, that shit y'all feeling in ya chest right now, that's that wolf. That's that 713. And the strength of the wolf is the strength of the pack. It's time to eat!" Slim barked.

Donovan nodded at Rico and then his brother, each showing a different understanding. He was done after this. There was a reason for him to be finally finished. He had Babygirl, the woman he loved. He might have been crazy for walking away from the only life he understood, but that didn't concern him. *If a man ain't willing to risk it all over a woman, then he's found the wrong woman,* he thought to himself, unafraid of his conviction. He looked at his best friend, his brother, and bumped fists with them.

"Time to hunt," Rico barked as the four men exited the vehicle.

K.T. parked the van behind the door and turned it around to exit at full speed if need be.

"Y'all um... Y'all said... ten minutes, right?" he asked nervously.

"Don't move the damn van until we're in it," Donovan barked, beating Slim to the punch of saying something more harsh.

As the van opened up, Donovan jumped out and scanned for the security cameras. They were dead.

"We're good. Let's move."

Rico, Trouble, and Slim headed for the door. Rico rushed to the lock and started working on it. He had been a part of a specialized unit in the navy where he had learned how to break locks in assisting the army with abducting high-value enemy combatants.

"Where are we, Rosey?" Slim asked quietly.

"Almost there," he said.

Donovan scanned the area. There was a chilling stillness in the air. He looked over at his friend, who was still tinkering with the keypad lock.

Slim leaned in and whispered, "We're against the clock, Rosey."

"Then shut the fuck up so I can work," he whispered back.

Donovan stepped towards the side of the van to get a good view of the main road, which was still quiet. He looked over at K.T. who was fidgeting. He then looked back at Slim hovering over Rico, who was still wrestling with the lock.

"Rosey."

"It's open."

Donovan jogged over to the side of the door as Rico prepared to open it. Rico lifted his hand to count.

Three... two... one.

Rico opened the door and Trouble and Slim entered the door, fully masked, followed by Donovan and Rico. The quartet walked into the back of the bank and turned to the first left. Sure enough, the security guard was asleep.

Donovan nodded to Rico to charge him before he had time to figure what was going on. He pulled the security guard to the front of the bank as Slim pulled out a digitized recording of himself and played it for the entire bank.

"Everyone put your hands in the air. If you listen, you'll live,"

The entire bank complied as Trouble secured the employees with Rico and waved the gun towards the second guard, signaling him to drop his gun.

The second guard hesitated, and Rico pressed the gun deeper into the first guard's neck, forcing him to kneel. This made the second guard lift his hands in the air slowly.

"Weapons and phones on the ground now!" the recording played next.

The guard slowly laid his weapon on the ground.

As Trouble and Rico secured the bank patrons, Donovan went to find the safe. Just like they had drawn it up, there was the cash. In fact, there were four extra bags. Without saying a word, Donovan lifted his left hand in the air, and Slim walked over as quietly as possible.

"There are 10 bags here, not 6."

"My man, Wonder Bread! He came through, didn't he?"

"We won't have room."

"We'll make room."

"Four extra bags is gonna take more time to load."

"Not as long as it's gonna take to have this discussion whether to take the bags or not."

"We don't have the room."

Slim walked over to the other side of the bank, where the men had rounded everyone up. He looked at the assistant bank manager and asked, "How much cash is back there?"

The assistant bank manager refused to answer the question. Slim took the back of his gun and broke his nose cleanly, causing blood to trickle onto the man's gray suit. He turned to the next employee.

"How much?"

"Five million. Please don't hurt me."

Slim walked back over to Donovan, who was already loading the cash.

"Five million. We'll make room. Take it all."

Donovan nodded. And loaded the van with Slim. They were on the fourth bag when the power spontaneously came back on. This distraction caught the gang off guard.

"The gate!" Trouble barked.

Donovan tuned to Slim. "We gotta go."

"One more bag."

Donovan rushed over to the back door. There was no van. K.T. had taken off with the money leaving the four of them to fend for themselves.

"Fuck!" he yelled. He ran back into the bank. He waved Trouble and Rico over and looked at Slim.

"Your boy is gone."

"What?"

"Let's bounce," he barked.

The four men exited the bank, unsure of what to do next.

Slim glanced at where the van should've been and banged his hand against the wall.

"That motherfucker. I can't believe it."

"I told you he was a coward."

"We gotta deal with that later. If we don't get out of this gate, we're all getting locked up. Trouble, get a car and we'll find that fucking van!"

"I'm on it," Trouble said as he ran off full speed.

The other three men scanned around.

We're not gonna make it carrying that cash," Donovan said.

Slim looked at the bag he was holding and dropped it. "Fuck. Alright let's go. We get to the next block, split up, meet at the spot."

The men started to run. They had made it to an alleyway the first block over when they heard it.

"Freeze! Don't move."

One of the restrained police officers had gotten free. He fired three rounds at the men, two of them missing and one of them hitting Slim as he returned fire, hitting the cop somewhere below the waist.

Donovan took off his mask. Slim's fool-proof plan was falling apart in front of his eyes. Donovan started rushing toward his brother when Rico pulled him back. He shrugged his best friend's hand off and sprinted towards his brother, who was lying on the ground bleeding from the abdomen. The rules didn't matter anymore. Slim was going to die if he didn't get help, something they both knew. He kneeled next to his brother, who waved him away.

"Hang on, Slim. Where are you hit? We gotta apply pressure!"

Slim exposed his wounds.

Donovan's previous estimation was wrong. All three rounds had hit Slim, causing him to bleed profusely.

"Ain't no amount of pressure gonna stop these leaks, Chop. You can't get this blood on you."

"I'm not leaving you! He—"

"Damn it, Chop! If you stay, we all going to die! I shot a cop. It's over for me. Get the fuck out of here. Spend that money. Get Rosey out of here. Make... Make it right, D."

Donovan ignored his brother and was about to put pressure on his would when Slim pointed this gun at him.

"I'm serious. Get the fuck out of here. Rosey, come get your boy."

Donovan felt Rico's hand on his shoulder.

"We can't just leave him here," Donovan said.

"You want to carry him, I'm with you, but we're not gonna make it, D. And... he's in no condition to get somewhere else."

"I'm not gonna make it either way, Chop. Get out of here, take the money. Go live."

Donovan looked at his brother. He knew everyone was right, but Slim was his brother. The last blood he had left. He looked at his best friend.

"Rosey, that time we were talking about... It's right now."

"Hermano."

"I'm not leaving Slim, but you gotta get out of here. Remember what you promised me."

Donovan watched his best friend, who silently nodded and then ran off. By leaving now, he had a good fighting chance of evading a police perimeter with the kind of traffic they were fighting against to get to the scene. Donovan wouldn't have much time at all. It didn't matter to him, though. Slim had little time on earth. Once Rico was out of sight, Donovan sat down next to his brother, still far enough away from the blood that was now spilling on the ground. He watched his brother smile as blood continued to pour from his body.

"Hey, Chop... Remember that time we washed Clive's car, and he took all of us to Astroworld?"

"Can't forget that day."

"Heh... he was so proud... braggin' to everybody. Me and you thought we could open a car wash business."

"Yeah... All you talked about for weeks was opening a car wash after that. I never understood why." Donovan replied.

"A car meant freedom... and a car wash in this hot ass city? I thought maybe, if we washed enough of them, we'd be able to get our own and get the hell out of there. Hell, maybe we'd be rich... Man, we made a lot of money that summer washing cars."

"Yeah, until we found out we could make even more money stealing the emblems off of the luxury cars."

"Ten dollars for a Caddy emblem and fifty for a Mercedes logo."

The pair laughed. Slim coughed up blood, but Donovan remained calm. They both knew Slim didn't have long.

"You know what I was gonna do with my money?"

"Nah... What did you have planned?"

"Open up our car wash. The Brown Boys' Car Wash and Detail. At least that's what I told myself, but... Maxine was right about me."

"You're nobody's rotten apple. You're my big brother, Darrion Brown."

"We both knew it was gonna end like this for me, Chop. If it wasn't today, then one day. I was never gonna stop. It was gonna catch up to me at some point. I'm not scared. I've been dead since I shot Clive."

Donovan looked his brother in his eyes. There was peace in them. Slim coughed up blood and smiled at him.

"Live your life your way, D. Fuck the 713 Boyz. Go be better than this... any of it. I'm sorry I couldn't protect you, Chop."

"You've always protected me, Slim. I need you to know that" Donovan said as tears ran down his face.

Slim smiled and nodded. He coughed violently with blood pouring from his mouth with each cough. "I'm gonna see mama, Chop. I'm so tired... I'm so tir—"

Donovan watched as his brother's eyes glazed over. He was gone. The pain would have paralyzed him if not for the sound of sirens. He knew he had to get up. *Come on, they're closing in, D. You gotta move... Now.* He stood up, forcing himself to block out the immeasurable pain that was running though his body. *One foot in front of the other. Run,* he told himself. Slowly, he began to run and eventually sprint. His instincts were returning to him. As much as he needed to grieve, now wasn't the time.

He hopped a fence and was in the back of a yard. He took off the utility uniform. Next, he found a storm drain and shoved the outfit and gun in the sewer before doubling back in the other direction. He was four blocks away when he ran out of steam. *Gotta find a car,* he thought to himself scanning the street frantically.

The sirens were everywhere. He was far enough away from the bank, but he had to get even further from the evidence.

Run, goddamn it. He pushed himself to the point of sweating profusely. The sirens were growing, gaining ground on him. He stopped running. The sirens grew to a deafening point. He was four blocks away from where he got rid of the evidence when he heard the two words he had been running from.

"Police! Freeze!"

Donovan turned around and was struck in the head by the butt of a gun, rendering him unconscious.

20
HARRIS COUNTY JAIL

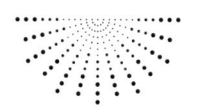

"Wake up, shit-head. It's time to go to the prom," Donovan heard as he opened his eyes.

"Where am I?" he whispered to himself. His head was throbbing. It was hard for him to remember anything. It wasn't until he felt the knot on his head that he remembered why. The stained aquamarine concrete bricks, the reverberating echoes that were now coming into focus, and the fact he had just been called a "shit-head" confirmed it. There was little doubt he was in a holding cell. He let out a groan as he felt the effects of several injuries that were undoubtedly the result of being worked over once he went unconscious. He could feel the trickle of blood from his scalp where the officer hit him in the head with the butt of the gun, and could taste blood in his mouth because of the same action. The stench of urine permeated the holding cell. As his eyes burned from the light and what had to be pepper spray, no doubt from some overzealous cop, he scanned the room. It was definitely a holding cell, and he realized he had been the only one apprehended. He sighed in relief. Trouble and Rico had made it.

"On your feet, asshole! I will not say it again," a clean shaven, heavyset white male with auburn hair barked.

"I'm moving, officer. Take it easy."

"Move now!"

Using what strength he had, he stood up and walked over to the gate, still groggy from being worked over. He glanced at the officer, who was talking to him, assuming he probably had something to do with his current aliments. Donovan was much larger than the man, and wasn't intimidated by his bravado. He also knew that his current state and predicament was the wrong place and time to do anything other than what he was told. For the time being anyway.

As the gate opened, he thought about the plan. Slim's fool-proof plan. The one that couldn't possibly go wrong. The one he should've known better than to follow.

It's on me... I broke the rules. The thought lingered in his head. The plan never had felt right to him, but he had convinced himself that he wanted the score deep down. His words to Rico echoed in his head. *Fool proof plans only prove that fools exist.* It bought him comfort hoping Rico was indeed free and that he had kept his word to Miss Gladys. *He'll be able to buy that house he's always yappin' about as long as he doesn't fuck up. Hell, maybe he'll actually go into comedy,* he thought.

No matter how much money they had got, the price was already too high, though. Slim was dead. His brother, the last member of his family. The image of him lying in the alleyway came jolting back to him. *The price was too damn high.*

He was feeling the gravity of it all, but he couldn't do that now, not while his own life was on the line. *Get your shit together or you're going to jail.* He calmly reminded himself he was already in the one place he was trying to avoid. The time for heartache and tears would have to wait. Now was the time to survive. Prison was something he'd known with a passing familiarity. Every male in his family had gone at some point. The problem was, it wasn't long from there that death would follow them. Slim was the latest victim of that.

Slim, his big brother, still lying in an alleyway. Probably still cold on the ground.

Donovan. Snap the fuck out of it, he commanded himself again. It wouldn't take much for his mind to drift. He had to concentrate. It was all part of the game until the price became too high. *If I can get out of this shit I'm done with it, I swear.*

He tried to direct his thoughts to someplace else. The car wash. The Brown Boys Car Wash and Detail. The last thing his brother had talked to him about. *Can't think about that now either,* he told himself. He had to keep his attention right where it was. Thinking in any other direction could cost him the next 25 years of his life. Right now, he had to figure out how to get out of this mess.

K.T.'s bitch ass ran, so as long as they didn't get Trouble or Rico, they can't have much, he thought to himself.

"I'll take it from here, Doug," another officer said.

A knot grew in the pit of Donovan's stomach as he glanced at the man who had said those words. *You gotta be shittin' me*, he thought to himself. His disbelief eroded any mental toughness he had built. He looked closer just to confirm his suspicion. Maybe his eyes were playing tricks on him. They weren't. *Motherfucking Columbo!* he screamed internally.

The cop who was taking custody of him was Officer Cunningham, the same one who had harassed him and Rico the night he met Nichelle. The night he had murdered Adrian Watson.

Shit! Do they know about that night? There's no way... They can't... How would they? Even if they had the crew, nobody would give that up, so how could they know? The security guard? The prostitute?

As his mind raced at the pace of 1000 miles an hour, he glanced at the officer again, who picked up on Donovan's gaze and in return took a closer look at him. He stopped and looked at his paperwork and then back at Donovan with a passing familiarity.

Shit, he knows, Donovan thought. He was in for a penny, but was about to pay a pound. He closed his eyes and sighed deeply as he walked. Now he could think about Nichelle. It was the only thing he had good left. *I fucked up*, he thought. His days of a free man were over.

"You got a problem?" the cop asked.

Donovan looked at the cop again. He'd seen this look before. The gaze of an officer wanting to instigate trouble, but gone was the look of any familiarity. He realized that the officer didn't remember him at all. He didn't know about the murder. This cop just enjoyed abusing his power. He turned away from the officer and continued to walk forward, slightly more settled than before.

"They worked you over real good, huh?" the officer said as he smiled in a manner that made Donovan feel like he was on the outside of an inside joke.

Donovan didn't respond. If he was going to jail for the rest of his life, he would not spend a moment of it being harassed by this asshole. The cop stopped and left him outside of a door in a line with men of a similar size and build. This wasn't the way things should be going. He'd never been in a lineup before, but he knew his attorney was supposed to be present. He turned back to the cop, who was walking away.

"Hey, ain't I supposed to have a lawyer present?"

"Quiet, asshole! Do as you're told."

"I'm asking for my law-"

Bam! The cop shoved him against the wall, sticking his baton against Donovan's throat. His airway was restricted, and he winced in pain as the officer barked at him.

"I said shut the hell up before I make you do so permanently."

Donovan said nothing.

The officer pressed the baton harder against his larynx.

Donovan resisted the urge to push him back. He knew any aggression would only escalate things. He glanced over in the area of a nearby camera and knew this was being recorded, something the officer hadn't considered.

Two other officers made their way down the hallway as the blood from Donovan's previous head wound started trickling from his head again.

"What in the fuck are you doing, Cunningham? You're gonna fuck up this case!" one officer yelled.

"I'm sorry. This asshole wouldn't stop talking."

"I just asked for... my lawyer," Donovan said, gasping for air. His voice was shot, no doubt because of the pressure just applied to his larynx.

Another officer pointed at him. "Hey, shut your damn mouth and go in the room."

Donovan said nothing else. In fact, for the first time, as bad as things were, he felt things were looking up. With his voice being gone and no one in the bank ever seeing his face, he knew the cop had just blown their best chance at a positive ID. He also knew that a cop with that much anger would've mentioned a murder and hadn't, so there was a good chance he was in the clear for the night of Adrian Watson's murder. All he had to do was fail the lineup with flying colors.

When he walked into the room, he leaned into the soreness in his voice. He was number three in the lineup, and as long as he didn't hear any knocks on the window, he was fine.

"Number one, step up and say, 'If you want to live, you won't be a hero today.'"

From the corner of his eye, Donovan could see a similarly built man step forward and repeat the line

"How much cash is back there?"

They had nothing. The man who had said those words was already dead. Donovan closed his eyes, trying to block out the pain of his brother being killed. He couldn't show that emotion now. It wouldn't take much to connect that Slim was his brother, but any emotion on his part would only strengthen their case.

He watched the first man in custody step back, having sounded nothing like his brother. He watched as they instructed the next man to perform the same task.

"How much cash is back there?"

Donovan knew it had to be the assistant bank manager. He couldn't see him, but he knew it was only him that was intimately familiar with Slim's voice. His brother, whom he sounded a lot like. He liked his chances less now.

"Number three, step forward and say the line."

Donovan hesitated. His freedom would be determined on what happened next.

"Number three!"

Donovan stepped forward. "How much cash is back there?"

His voice cracked several times in the short sentence. He didn't sound at all like himself and thus nothing like Slim. At least in his opinion, but his opinion wasn't the one that mattered at this moment.

There was a long pause. Donovan was hoping they'd move on when the PA system came back on again.

"Number three, step forward and say the line again, but louder!"

Fuck! he thought to himself. Maybe his voice wasn't as badly damaged as he'd thought. He took a deep breath, stepped forward, and delivered the line again. "How much cash is back there?"

He strained through the sentence the second time. There was no way he sounded like himself. Another brief pause ensued. He wondered if the woman had identified him outside. Maybe this was all for show.

"Number four, step forward and say the line."

The man sounded intimidating, and he was also bigger than him. A wave of relief rushed over him. There was no way to be certain, but he sensed there wasn't a positive ID, and that meant the state was playing with all circumstantial evidence. They had nothing.

After the final two men repeated the line, they were all escorted out. They were walking to the holding cell when officer Cunningham walked up to the officer standing with Donovan and whispered in his ear.

"Change of plans. We're going to interrogation room F."

21
NOW I FEEL YA

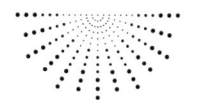

The interrogation room was intentionally colder than the rest of the building. This was a deliberate police tactic to make a suspect uncomfortable and wear them down mentally, assuming that many of the suspects in custody would be accustomed to the sweltering Texas heat.

The fact that he was here instead of in a holding cell told Donovan two things, the first of which was, he was definitely a suspect, and the second was, he'd be here for a while. The officer pinned his hand to the metal latch that was connected to the steel metal desk, slamming his wrist against the table, causing him to wince in pain.

"My bad, home boy," the cop mocked him as he kept his focus on the door.

There were clusters of police officers gathering in the hallway and they were all just looking for a reason to pounce on him and he knew it. Donovan wasn't sure how much they knew, or what he was being charged with, but he knew he needed to react as little as possible.

The light positioned directly above his head was far too bright considering his head was still pounding and bleeding. Donovan wiped the wound with the back of his free hand to stop it from trickling onto the table. He wanted water and a cigarette, but that would not happen. In fact, any help from anyone in a uniform could only involve getting his ass kicked while cuffed.

If there was one thing that worked to his advantage, it was that he was comfortable waiting for long periods of time, since it was a critical part of his line of work. Yet, with a mind-numbing headache and at least two possibly broken ribs, he was already mentally exhausted.

Stay strong, Chop.

He could hear the remnants of his brother's voice echo in his mind as his arms developed goosebumps from the room's growing chill. *Can't afford to think about that now,* he reminded himself.

He was three hours into what felt like an endless wait. By hour six, he thought about her. She would be off by now and he wasn't there. He wasn't sure what she knew or didn't know, but he knew one unmistakable truth. He should've never left her side this morning.

Can't go there, D. Gotta focus. Damn... I could use a smoke right now, he thought.

Tap. Tap.

The door opened, and the officer walked in accompanied by a reasonably tall, very attractive, light cinnamon complected woman in a crimson skirt suit. Donovan recognized her clothing as similar to Nichelle's, which meant it was expensive. He watched as she walked to the chair and waited for the cop, whose initial bravo was now absent, as he scurried to accommodate the woman.

She waited until the officer pulled out her chair, and as she sat, without a word, the same officer pushed her closer to the table. She waved her hand, and the cop left the room, closing the door behind him. Whether it was a parlor trick to get him to feel intimidated, or she was actually that influential, the message was received. She was in charge.

Now facing Donovan without a word, she took her glasses, which were hanging on the collar of her jet-black silk top, and placed them on the brim of her nose before opining the case file. She read it quietly. After a spell, she closed the file and looked at Donovan.

"Mr. Brown, I'm District Attorney Alexandria Hughes, and by the end of this conversation, I promise you, I'm going to do you a favor and will have earned your trust." Her confidence was as cold as the room they were both sitting in.

He studied her carefully to determine any weak spots in her mannerisms or if she would tip her hand in a conversation. He leaned in close and replied to her with one word.

"Lawyer."

"One step at a time, Mr. Brown. We're just getting to know each ot—."

"Law-yer," he repeated. He would not talk, and he wanted to make sure she knew it.

She calmly leaned back and pulled out a pack of Camel cigarettes. She lit one and took a puff. It was his brand. The only brand he smoked. He looked into her eyes and she locked in on his. In an unspoken language, she told him, *I know more about you than you think.* She put the cigarette out and left the pack on the table.

"You remember that first promise I made you? Here." She slid the pack of cigarettes over to him along with the lighter.

Donovan looked at her blankly.

She smirked at his reaction. "Mr. Brown, the time to be worried about crossing lines was... well, many lines ago. One more isn't gonna hurt, I promise."

Without saying a word, he took the cigarettes and lit one, taking a long drag. As he began to exhale, Alexandria used the key to unlock his hand from the chair, surprising him, but only partly. Camels were the brand of cigarette he'd been smoking since he started smoking. Could it be a coincidence? He wanted to know how she knew what brand of cigarettes he smoked, but he knew the less he said the better.

The woman stretched and smiled. "You know, people may believe my job is to catch whoever did it and put them away... and that would be partially true, but priority one is that I win. I love that about my job because I'm extremely good at it. These interrogation rooms just make my pussy all warm and creamy inside. And I mean that literally. I get off on this shit. I'm not sure why, and it's probably a problem, but, despite it all, I know one thing: I'm not going to ever get fucked the way whoever's responsible for this crime will be by the city."

The door opened and a man, presumably the lawyer Donovan had been asking for, stuck his head in.

Alexandria turned to look at him. "They sent Andy!" she exclaimed.

The lawyer hesitated, looking at Donovan and then back at Alexandria. "H... hi Alex."

"Donovan Brown, this is Andrew Blanchard, but everybody calls him Forgetful Andy because he's always forgetting an important piece of information in his cases."

"No one calls me that but you."

"Are you sure? Or did you forget?" she said, beaming from ear to ear.

Her confidence made Donovan uneasy. He looked at the attorney, a middle-aged portly white male with auburn hair and freckles, wearing a cheap stone-colored suit and brown shoes. A complete contrast in every way to the woman who was all but salivating like a wolf finding a defenseless lamb. He watched as Alex chuckled.

"You know, he's right. I have nicknames for all those little guys down there. They're so funny and harmless. If it were me, I wouldn't trust any of them with my grocery list, let alone my freedom, but judging by your non-existent bank records, you can't afford an attorney now, can you? Unless.... you so happen to have come into some windfall of cash today."

"Nice try, Alex, but my client isn't admitting to anything."

She looked at the new attorney and smiled. "You know, the second thing I promised you is I'd be honest. Trust me, you do not want this guy for a lawyer."

"Alex, you can't do this. I'm no—"

"Andy, answer these questions for your client. How many times have we been head-to-head?"

"Alex..."

"Your client should know that."

Donovan looked at the lawyer as if to give him permission to answer the question.

He turned red as he responded to her. "Seven.... We've been head-to-head on a case seven times."

"And how many times have you won a case against me?"

"None."

"In fact, how many times have any of your guys in that little defense attorney's club won a case against me?"

"None."

"Andy, can you tell your client what my nickname is down there in your little hall of justice... the one you won't dare to call me to my face?"

Donovan watched his lawyer tense up behind the notion that Alex was aware of the way they talked about her behind her back.

Andy responded. "We... we call you the judge."

"And why is that?"

"Because... when you're on the case... It's already been decided."

"And last question. What's your client's name?"

"I... uh..."

She turned to Donovan and smirked. Her face read, "I told you so," as the lawyer ruffled through his files.

Donovan couldn't show it, but it dismayed him how easily she had disposed of his would-be attorney. He glanced at Alex, who continued.

"Look at him, Mr. Brown. Do you see the defeat in his eyes? I put that there a while ago. You don't want this man in charge of your freedom. You can go now, Andy. We won't be needing you."

Andy looked over at Donovan and then back at Alex. "He... has... to fire me."

Alexandria looked at Donovan, who was in disbelief about the entire exchange.

"Yeah, get the fuck out of here, man."

The lawyer got up and scrambled, dropping his files, but then picking them up and exiting.

"Now, Mr. Brown. Where were we?"

22
BEST WORST DAY

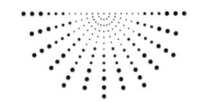

"So now that you've pulled your dick out to show everyone you're packing a big one, when do I get my next lawyer?" Donovan asked her as he smoked another one of the Camel cigarettes.

She stood up and leaned over in front of him. "I know you don't trust me, Mr. Brown, but by the time I'm finished saying what I'm about to tell you, I promise I will have earned your trust. And when I pull my dick out, you'll know it."

Unphased, Donovan blew smoke in the woman's face, who smiled and took the cigarette from his mouth and placed it in her own lips, seductively taking a drag before sensually placing it back in his lips.

What in the fuck is this lady on? he thought to himself. He knew these were all tactics to catch him off balance, yet they were actually working. This was not the way anything had ever gone with him when dealing with law enforcement. For the first time since he'd been detained, he was uneasy.

Alex circled back around to the front of his chair. "Speaking of dicks, I have to say I am curious... I'm pretty sure you're packing some lumber, aren't you? What's in those britches 9... 10 inches?"

"Lady, where in the fuck is my lawy—"

"Eleven? No way you got an eleven-inch dick."

Donovan ashed the cigarette on the table. It was time to go on the offense.

"If you're so worried about my dick, why don't you come over and see for yourself? If you're not going to do that, get me my goddamn lawyer."

Alex got up off of the table and, without a word, walked to stand in front of him and dropped to her knees. Her eyes dripped with sexual energy as she parted her lips ever so slightly before turning her attention to his crotch area. She slowly licked her lips while gazing at him. Her lustful gaze made him uncomfortable, but was slowly arousing him. She was dripping with sexual energy, and while he wasn't confused about where he was and what was happening in the slightest, he was being dragged into her aura.

His manhood began to rise. He looked at her, salivating as he tried to resist her sensual nature. His body betrayed him for the second time as his pants began to bulge. He turned away from her, facing the door.

"Lady, you are crazy as shit," he said as he moved himself and the chair away from her.

"Ten and a half inches. Very nice...," she said as she stood up. She sat back down and put her glasses back on. "That's enough fun and games. Let's get down to brass tax. I'm gonna tell you how policing works. You're almost 12 hours into a window of 24 hours since stealing 2 million dollars, and the police don't have a goddamn clue where the money is. We don't have any physical evidence, nor do we have any video footage. The eye witness to the crime couldn't pick you out of a lineup, and I don't think you're going to tell us anything anytime soon. So, in just a few brief hours, under normal circumstances, this case would be closed. The problem for you, at least, is your brother or someone, shot a cop."

Donovan watched as Alex took one last glance at this crotch, shook her head and then looked back at him.

"So, your problem becomes the media. The news is going to ask about the condition of said cop. Who, from what I hear will pull through, by the way, but not any time soon. They are going to interview his wife and show pictures of his kids, and all of this is just going to piss the locals off. The media is going to feed into that and keep pumping more stories, so while we're waiting on the officer's condition to get better, you know what else they're going to ask?"

"Nah, what?" he said mockingly.

"Have you caught any other suspects? Well, all we have is you, and if we let you go, then we're going to have to say, 'We're still investigating.' Which means we will actually have to keep investigating because eventually the media will start asking the mayor, and he's going to say something along the lines of, 'We need our citizens safe. Justice prevails.' Blah, blah, blah, you get the idea. So, while all of that is going on, you'll be back in custody as they rip apart every single thread in the fabric that is your life because we'll have the full authority and resources of the city of Houston to go after you. If there is just one thread that you haven't knitted tightly, then it's all going to come unraveled. I'll win this case regardless, though, because your brother was found dead at the scene and the world doesn't care what happens to the relative of a dead, black bank robber who shot a cop."

Donovan knew her logic made sense. They wouldn't stop looking. He focused his eyes on Alex to see if she was lying or not. His skill for reading people returned a haunting revelation. She was telling him the truth.

Alex continued. "On the other hand. You could plead 'no contest' to a lesser charge of aggravated assault, do seven years, with good behavior making that about three and a half, and the media will have their story. The mayor, and thus the city, gets their happily ever after story, and when you get out of jail, you'll have 2 million dollars you can spend, provided you're as good as I think you are. Because the truth is, no one cares about the money either. The bank has already filed the insurance claim. The only thing that matters here is your choice. The choice is yours to make. This is just me and you and if you plead 'no contest,' there won't be any questions asked."

"And why would I be so lucky to get this kind of deal if what you say is true?"

"Because I don't give a shit about this job anymore. This is my last case. The sooner I close it out, the faster I get to my next cushy six figure job. But rest assured, I will win it."

Alex pulled a bottle of water from her briefcase and took a sip. She then handed the bottle to Donovan, who had had nothing to drink or eat since he left Nichelle this morning. The room was chilly. He was beaten physically and emotionally exhausted. He took a sip of the water and responded.

"'Thanks, lady, but I think with the weak evidence you have, it might be worth getting it dismissed outright."

Alex shook her head like a disapproving parent and took another sip of the water bottle.

"Mr. Brown, do you know that the conviction rate for the average lawyer is somewhere between 63 and 72 percent? My conviction rate is 97.3. The highest in the history of the district attorney's office, and that has entitled me to get a job at one of the most prestigious law firms in the city. My point is, this is my last case, Mr. Brown, and I honestly don't care who goes down for it, but rest assured, someone is going down for it. In fact, I have it on good authority you'll end up in Judge Abrams' court for this one, and he presides with the good ole boy fashioned racism you've come to expect in this town. In fact, the one thing I know about that judge is he's a sexist and racist piece of shit. He wishes all of us minorities were in our proper roles, whatever that means. In fact, the only thing he's hates more than a confident woman is a big lipped thug that can't respect the law. He also gets a rigid hard on for anyone who harms a cop. I know as much because I recorded him saying those exact words about three weeks ago. I made the recording to leverage that information in order to land the high six-figure job that I'm leaving this one for."

He wasn't sure what to make of her or what she was saying. The one thing he did know was when a person felt they had nothing to lose, they were dangerous. He decided to go on the offensive and tip his hand.

"Why are you telling me this? I'll bring all of this up as soon as the next lawyer walks in the door." Alexandria smiled and sighed as she looked at her nail polish.

"You could, but who would believe you? A suspect accused of robbing a bank and shooting a cop versus the word of a District Attorney and a judge who's been on the bench for 26 years? Besides, you saw what I did to the last lawyer and I haven't even gotten my nails done. Honey, when I'm in that courtroom, looking as good as I look, do you think anyone is going to hear anyone else?"

Donovan was silent. She was extremely attractive and clearly confident in her abilities. There was a good chance she was right about what she'd just said. He sipped the water as she continued.

"Now, you probably live by some ass backwards code about not snitching, looking out for da homies or whatever you guys tell yourselves these days. The point I'm making is, you're a speed bump in the wheels of justice, so when I tell you taking this deal is the only way out of this that doesn't unleash holy hell on your life, you'd better believe me. This is a once in a lifetime deal. This is your best day ever. Don't make it your worst."

Alex sat down in her chair, opened the file to pull out some paperwork and slid the sheets over to him. "This is the deal I'm offering. All you have to do is sign."

Donovan glanced at the paperwork and then away toward the wall. Another lawyer walked through the door. Alex chuckled and crossed her legs as the lawyer fumbled through his paperwork.

The middled-aged white male looked at Donovan and asked, "Umm, are you Marquis? Attempted car jacking?

"Donovan. Donovan Brown."

"I'm sorry. This just landed on my desk and it's my 12th case for the week," the lawyer said.

Alex lifted an eyebrow and glanced over at Donovan. "You really want to roll the dice with this one?"

Donovan let out an enormous sigh and rolled his eyes. He thought about her words. They weren't asking for any of the details of the crime. They had nothing, but at the same time, Alexandria was right.

She was going to devour this lawyer just like she did the last one. The longer this went on, the longer they would look for the rest of the crew too. He could end it all, right here, right now. He grabbed the paper that was sitting on the desk and examined it while his new would-be lawyer sorted through his own papers, still trying to figure out who he was representing.

After a spell, Donovan said, "I'm not admitting nothing, but if I took this deal, what would that look like?"

"You plead 'no contest' and I'll take it from there."

"I need more than 'I'll take it from there.' You said you wanted me to trust you. Now's that time, counselor. If I sign this... Are you done?" Alex leaned in and looked him firmly in the eyes.

"The City of Houston will formally close the books on this investigation and, barring you don't do something else stupid while you're inside, you'll serve three and a half years tops."

Donovan looked at his lawyer, who was still unsure who he was. The man took the paperwork, examined it, and nodded to show that the deal looked legally binding.

Regardless of what she said, one thing was true. The police wouldn't stop looking for them if the story stayed in the news cycle. He also knew by them being this desperate that they had nothing. But, more than anything, he'd promised Miss Gladys that Rico wouldn't go back to jail if he could at all help it. A half a million each was worth three years. *Babygirl... Damn it.* She wouldn't understand. She had known something was off, yet he hadn't listened to her. He wanted to tell her the words she'd been looking to hear, words her heart already knew. He loved her deeply. But for now, he'd have to take one for the team. Donovan looked at Alexandria and took a deep sigh.

"I want one of those deals you give the white boys where you get the night to get your affairs in order."

"You are out of your rabbit-ass mind, Mr. Brown."

"Lady look, you want me to trust you? This is me trusting you. I'm signing this paper, but I didn't do this crime. I just know you're good. If all you told me is true, I'd be a fool to do anything else. You have my word. I'll be back in the morning."

She nodded in agreement, and then placed a pen on top of the paper and looked him square in his eyes. "There," she said, placing the pen firmly in front of him. Steeling her voice, she unflinchingly continued, "Now, my dick's on the table. Pick it up and sign."

Her words cut like a serrated blade against the skin of his forearm. He'd learned growing up in the streets of Houston if someone was lying, in that brazen moment they would flinch. She was as cold as he was, unmoved by any of it. There were no legal parlor tricks. Every word of what she'd just said had been the truth. Her tone and manner forced him to accept that she was indeed doing him a favor, one that benefited the both of them. He also knew that he was guilty of the crime, and it would only be a matter of time before the other dominoes fell if he stood in her way. This was his one and only chance to close the investigation. Three years would be worth half a million dollars if no one made a mistake. He looked at Alex and picked up the pen.

"If I sign this, that's the end of it?" he asked

"The City of Houston will officially close the case. I'll even give you the rest of the day to get your affairs in order. But, if you make me work? If you're not here in the morning at 7:59, I will make this unpleasa—."

"I get it."

Fuck. I'm sorry, Babygirl, he thought to himself. Of all the things that had gone wrong today, he'd at least get to tell her himself. And despite how much he wanted to tell her how he had changed and that he loved her with all of his heart, the worst parts of his nature had come back to haunt him. It wasn't worth punishing her further by asking her to wait on him, but he was grateful for one last night with his Babygirl. He wasn't sure why this lawyer was in his presence. He knew all of this was unconventional, but this was indeed his best, worst day.

He signed his name and handed the paper back to Alexandria. "So, what now?"

"Well, now that we have an understanding, you're free to go. But I implore you, don't make me work on my last day. Not to put too fine a point on it, but if I have to find you, I'm going to start with your surrogate mother, and I'm sure you wouldn't want these officers to show her the same hospitality they showed you today."

Donovan cautiously nodded in agreement. It was tempting to make a run for it but running for the rest of his life would only result in more heartache for everyone, and there had been enough of that for one day. He stood up, eager to spend his final night as a free man with the person he loved the most. He extended his hand to the smirking woman in front of him. "I'll be here in the morning."

The End.

HERE'S A SNEAK PEAK AT THE NEXT NOVEL- MONEY, POWER & SEX: A LOVE STORY

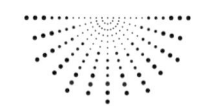

The Response

IT WAS 6:30 IN THE EVENING. LUCAS WAS JUST GETTING HOME FROM A long day's work and was ready to unwind for the evening. Before he walked in the house, he let his dogs out of the garage. The weather had been dreadful the past week—every day below thirty, which was odd for Texas, but particularly Houston.

The weatherman's forecast had been for about twenty degrees warmer than it actually was, but Lucas, being a native of the city, wasn't really surprised that the forecast had been that far off.

AccuWeather, my ass, he thought as he petted his oldest dog, a full-blooded black lab named Nightcrawler. He'd taken a liking to the dog because of his jet-black coat when he found him as a pup at a shelter. Lucas, being 5'11" with a comparable dark-chocolate complexion, found the dog similar in nature to himself—compassionate, playful, and intelligent. He knew they'd get along once he named him Nightcrawler after *The X-Men* comic book character, and he wasn't wrong. The two had been great companions ever since.

On the other hand, Mika, his newest dog, had been abused by her previous owner before Lucas found her at the same shelter. Lucas had yet to win Mika's affection, but decided to leave her to her own devices until she finally came around in her own time.

As he slipped his key into the lock, his cellphone rang. Looking at the caller ID brought a big smile to his face. "Hey, you! How you doing?"

A soft, sensual voice on the other end responded, "Hey, baby! You home already?"

The world around him became warmer the moment Lucas heard Nichelle's voice. "Yeah, I'm home. How was work today?"

"You won't believe what happened," Nichelle replied. "You know that crazy lady I'm always telling you about? Well, you won't believe what she had the nerve to say to me today!"

Smiling on his way to the kitchen, Lucas said, "Oh, boy! I can't even begin to imagine what Ms. Patrice has going on."

Lucas took off his coat and turned on the kitchen light as Nichelle dove into her story—one Lucas knew all too well. Ms. Patrice had been working on Nichelle's nerves for the past year or so. She complained about everything from the other employees to why she wouldn't eat cantaloupe, but Patrice's current focus was on the recently ended review process—and Patrice was pissed. Not only was she upset, but she wanted everyone to know, especially Nichelle.

Nichelle continued. "So Patrice was just leaving my desk, and our coworker, James, was behind her as they walked into the kitchen, right? Now, you'd *think* the woman would hold the door open for him because he had both hands full, but this heifer slams the door in his face! When I asked her why, she was like, 'I'm a lady, so he should always open doors for me!'"

Nichelle was laughing so hard she sounded on the verge of tears as she continued her story. Lucas was laughing just as hard as he cut up the onions, the final ingredient for his entrée. He was making baked chicken stuffed with bits of turkey bacon, cheese, green onions, mushrooms, and a hint of garlic—prepared specifically for Nichelle.

"I don't mean to interrupt, baby, but how far are you from my house?" Lucas asked.

Nichelle replied, "Probably about thirty minutes with all this traffic. You know people don't know how to drive down here when it's cold, and they *sure* don't know how to drive when it's raining—and today it's cold *and* raining... so make it forty-five."

"Perfect," Lucas said.

The chicken would need thirty minutes to cook, and his sides of sweet potatoes and a broccoli and cheese casserole would need twenty minutes. He wanted to make sure the sweet potatoes were soft and the casserole cooled to the right temperature.

As they continued their conversation, Lucas went outside to get some firewood. He had acquired a stockpile of large- and medium-sized wood after he helped in the relief effort following Hurricane Patricia. He had anticipated burning the wood, but Nichelle called him crazy for doing it, considering the weather in Houston hardly ever got really cold. He decided to use this opportunity not only to heat the house and set the mood, but to make an "I told you so" point.

As Nichelle continued telling him about her day, Lucas interjected affectionately, "I miss you."

His heartfelt remark paused the conversation. It was filled with all the potency and weight of his meaning—and Nichelle understood his words perfectly. He couldn't wait to get his arms around her and draw her into one of those passionate kisses they shared so frequently. It was as if time lost all meaning when their lips met.

Some people throw their words around like Frisbees, but Lucas wasn't one of them. He was meticulous about his words to deliver his precise meaning. Nichelle admired the way he used his words.

In return, she filled her own words with fervor. However simple they might be, they were equal to his in value. "Baby, I miss you too."

At that moment, the silence was so dense that their individual thoughts carried them to the same place. The moment could've gone on for hours as they thought about what each wanted to do with the other. How they'd kiss, enjoy each other's scent, and touch each other tenderly.

As those thoughts snowballed, something unusual took place in the city of Houston. It began to snow, which brought both of them back to reality.

"Lucas, it's snowing out here!" Nichelle screamed.

"That's insane!" Lucas responded, still outside, loading his arms with firewood. "Hurry home. I've got a little something planned. In fact, I'm going to get off the phone right now so I can make the final preparations."

"Well, go ahead, Mr. Man. I don't want to hold you."

"Nichelle, before you go," Lucas added, "do you remember the question you asked me the other day? Well, I have an answer for you. I'll tell you when I see you."

As Nichelle tapped her phone off, she searched her memory for the question Lucas mentioned—and it made her giggle. Two days earlier, they'd been at Mike and Divia's house playing team Scrabble when Lucas ended up getting the winning word—a word she'd been having a hard time finding: value.

Beating the other couple prompted Nichelle to ask Lucas, "You bring so much value to my life, boo. What do I bring to yours?"

In response, Lucas said half-jokingly, "Let me think about it."

She should've known he was being literal—it was just his style. He was a man who stood behind his words. A good man—tall, dark, handsome, sexy, funny, smart—and he was all hers.

As she came up with more adjectives to describe Lucas, Nichelle's fingers slowly slid down to her crotch, and she almost lost sight of the road in front of her. The mere thought of that man turned her on. She could only imagine what he had in store for her when she got to his house. He was always full of surprises. She wanted him inside her, and the closer she got to his home, the more she wanted him.

Her panties began to grow moist the moment they first got on the phone, and she was finding it hard to concentrate. It seemed that no matter how cold it was outside, it was heating up inside the car. By the time she made it to the subdivision, she had worked herself up to the point where she was eager to practice her cowgirl skills.

After she parked her black Audi A5 in the driveway, she checked herself out in the rearview mirror and applied a fresh coat of her favorite lip gloss, *Petal,* by Bobbi Brown. She then adjusted her C-cup bra and took a deep breath. For the last forty-five minutes, the moisture that had been building in her panties had developed into a borderline gush. She was aching to get inside, peel off her clothes, and be pounded into submission.

She was so wet that it was hard to walk as her thighs glided from lubrication. There was no doubt in her mind that when she opened the door, Lucas would claw at her in an urgent attempt to get her into her birthday suit.

She scurried through the gate and fiddled with her keys to open the back door. Before she could slide her key into the lock, the door opened, startling her slightly, since the back hallway light wasn't on.

Lucas was at the door. Nichelle dropped her B. Makowsky purse in the hallway, slammed the door behind her, and kissed Lucas furiously, as if his lips were water in a dry desert. Lucas explosively returned the kiss, embracing her and pressing his body firmly against hers.

That kiss was only the beginning of what Nichelle had in mind. She could feel every inch of Lucas's manhood rising in his pants, so it startled her when he suddenly pulled away.

"What are you doing, baby?" she asked with concern and slight irritation.

"We have to wait," Lucas responded halfheartedly.

"Lucas, I'm in no mood to play," Nichelle said as she rubbed her hand over his erection.

"Believe me, baby, I don't want to play either," Lucas said, "but I told you I have something planned, and we—"

"I know, baby, but could you just fuck me really hard first, and then do what you have planned?"

It was an offer that Lucas didn't want to turn down, but he knew that as kinky as having sex in the hallway might be, they had all night, and eventually they could fuck their way back to that spot. "Nichelle, baby, I promise I'll make up for it," he said. "Please, come with me."

"Fine," she responded, her voice dripping with disappointment.

Only then did she realize that not only were the hallway lights off, but the only light she could see looked like candlelight glittering in the dimness of the dining room. As she wrestled her horniness into a corner, she smelled the scent of cinnamon-baked sweet potatoes, turning her grumpiness into curiosity. Her mood elevated even more when she realized there was a delicate trail of pink, red, and white rose petals leading to the kitchen.

Lucas led her by the hand, and as they entered the dining room, she saw a candlelit table containing a bottle of Yamhill-Carlton, one of her favorite pinot noir wines, and a three-course meal. The dinner looked and smelled as if it were prepared by Aida Mollenkamp herself, and her glass of wine sat poured and waiting.

"Surprise," Lucas said softly. "If you're ready, baby, let's eat."

Unable to speak, all Nichelle could do was sit, eat, and be astonished. She knew he had been planning something, but she never anticipated this.

The food was perfect; the ambiance heightened by what seemed to be a never-ending stream of her favorite songs—everything from *Let It Snow* by Boyz II Men and Brian McKnight to *Love TKO* by Teddy Pendergrass. By the time Ray Charles's *Baby, It's Cold Outside* came on, the only meat Nichelle wanted in her mouth was the one in Lucas's pants. It was a double-edged sword. Lucas could turn her on, but Nichelle was so impatient once she got going that she didn't want to wait—ever. His self-control was an enigma to her.

"Lucas, I want you—now!" Nichelle said breathlessly.

"Baby, you know I want you, too, but before we go there—and I *promise* we'll go there—I have one more thing I want to give to you."

"Is it in your pants?" Nichelle asked with a wink.

Lucas smiled and replied, "Not just yet."

"Lucas—" Nichelle said impatiently. She was excited to see what he had in store for her, but she was horny as a toad and didn't know how much longer she could deny her inner freak.

Lucas smiled again at her impatience and said, "But it *does* require you to take off your clothes, so if you wouldn't mind, I need you to strip."

That last word couldn't have sounded sexier at that moment, and Nichelle was instantly down with the idea of getting naked, yet she still wondered why he needed her to be naked while not mentioning anything about making love. Whatever it was really didn't matter. She began to take off her clothes, since it was definitely a step in the right direction.

As Nichelle unbuttoned her crème-colored Ralph Lauren blouse and slid out of her charcoal Jones of New York slacks, she heard Lucas whisper, "Oh, damn."

Looking at Nichelle's 5-foot-3, silky-smooth caramel frame enclosed in a black satin Victoria's Secret bra-and-panty set, Lucas wondered why he'd been torturing himself for so long. The candlelight flickered on her skin, as if conforming to her natural shapeliness. Her body would have made a goddess feel inadequate, and "Oh, damn" was all he could muster at the moment.

She teased him slightly as she removed her bra, and in spite of himself, the way her breast popped out reminded him of a jack-in-the-box. Her breasts were so firm and perky that the bra was really just for show—and he couldn't wait to lick them.

As she slid off her black satin thong, Lucas was rock hard again, staring at the buildup of wetness clinging to her panties. He wanted to lick her where her moisture lived. He extended his hand to her now fully naked body and led her into the bedroom.

As he opened the door, she noticed the smirk on his face when she glanced at the fireplace next to the large window and saw an unspoken "I told you so." Lucas wasn't the type of brotha to let it go unmentioned, so Nichelle decided to beat him to the punch.

"So you got to use some of your firewood," she said with a sly smile. "Con—"

The word would've been *Congratulations* if the cat hadn't gotten her tongue at that moment. Sitting in front of her was a massage table and what appeared to be one of the most inclusive masseuse tool kits she'd ever seen.

"Okay, baby, just lay on the table and relax," Lucas said softly.

He was definitely in control of the evening, and she instantly understood his plan. His mission was to give her the full-service treatment, which she often referred to as the three F's: Feeding, Foreplay, and Fucking.

"I want you to just relax and enjoy this," Lucas said.

She did what he suggested, and then Lucas poured a mint oil extract onto her body to open her pores. Her muscles, tense from her sex drive, yielded to his will as he rubbed the oil onto her body. By the time he applied the butter crème wax, she had nearly orgasmed from sheer pleasure. He had mentioned this before, but she never had the pleasure of having wax applied to her body. It was warm as he applied it generously—the most marvelous thing she had ever felt.

The crème began to harden around the tense areas of her body, though it was still soft enough for his fingers to apply added pressure to her muscles. The only thing she could do was moan with pleasure as his hands worked her entire body, from her shoulder blades to her spine, from her waist to her plump bottom, from her thighs to her calves, and all the way back to her shoulders again.

"Lucas, baby," she said dreamily.

She didn't have to finish her request. Lucas knew it was time to give her what she'd been wanting all night. What they both wanted—each other.

"You ready for me, baby?" he whispered gently in her ear.

Nichelle could scarcely make out what he said. She had been so consumed with pleasure that she felt drugged. He'd brought her to the height of ecstasy without ever going inside her. She struggled to regain control of her senses as he pulled the hardened wax off her body. Only then did she realize that he was completely naked, too. He must've taken his clothes off at some point during the massage, but his hands felt so good she couldn't remember when.

Lucas had been waiting for this moment since he'd left her side the night before. He picked her up and laid her gently on the bed, then kissed her navel, working his way down her right thigh, picking up intensity as he moved into the center of her legs. Her clitoris was fully exposed and firm. He began to write the alphabet with his tongue, as if her clit were his notepad.

"A, B, C…"

Nichelle's inner freak had met its match, and Lucas wasn't playing around.

"G, H, I…"

His tongue bounced her clit around like a speed bag by time he got to "O," which ironically was when her body began to shake with an intense orgasm.

"Now let's set it off," Lucas said as he climbed on top of her.

She looked into his light-brown eyes and welcomed his body into hers. She'd been waiting for hours for him to give her his massive rod, and now it was finally going to happen.

For Lucas, it was like entering a temple. He had already been on his knees in worship; now he was about to enter the sanctuary.

Nichelle couldn't believe what she was feeling. Each thrust filled her with a completely new sensation. He was so firm, so thick, and so intense that her pussy felt as if it were being stretched each time he stroked in and out of her body.

His penis continued to rub against her G-spot, and like the massage, it broke down her tension, sending Nichelle's body into a stream of multiple orgasms. He plunged so deep inside her with each thrust that she gasped with pleasure, as if breathing for both of them.

The lovemaking lasted for hours. Nichelle came so many times that she could no longer recall when or how many times they switched positions. Each time she tried to put it on him, Lucas returned the favor by bringing her to another climax. When she found herself in the middle of one of the most mind-bending orgasms she'd ever experienced, Lucas finally reached his own climax. Her nails dug deep into his skin, but she couldn't have cared less as he moaned savagely, filling her vagina with a massive dose of his sweet, sticky semen.

His eyes then glazed over, letting her know he could go no more. He was as satisfied as she was—but a dozen times over. As they lay together in the darkness, Nichelle put her head on Lucas's chest, feeling his solid physique. She wiped away a final tear of pleasure, then sighed deeply, as if trying to catch her breath for the first time in hours.

"Happiness," Lucas whispered.

"Huh?" Nichelle asked, not sure if she heard him correctly.

"Happiness," Lucas whispered again. "The value you bring to my life is happiness. It's my pleasure to *serve* you."

She looked up at him and found serenity in his eyes. The entire night had been about catering to *her* needs. He took joy in pleasing her.

Laying silently in his loving arms, Nichelle wondered if there was any limit to Lucas's amazingness. She even wondered if he had somehow managed to make it snow, just to make the night more memorable. He knew she loved snow, even though it never snowed in Houston. Had he somehow worked a miracle? She wouldn't have put it past him. Not at this moment. After all, this cold winter night had been nothing short of perfect.

ABOUT THE AUTHOR

Norian Love is a best-selling author, screen-writer, songwriter, and poet, whose character-rich storytelling and creative world-building is swiftly setting him apart as one of the top writers in the black romance genre. His latest release, Autumn: A Love Story, was the recipient of the Association of Black Romance Writers 2021 Book of the Year Award. Autumn's complementary poetic journal, Blue: Love Letters to Fatima, also became a number one best-seller, giving him the unique distinction of having number one releases across multiple genres. He was a finalist for the 2021 Black Authors Rock, Author of the Year Award, as well as a finalist for the 2022 Romance Slam Jam Best Erotic Romance EMMA Award. He is working on completing the highly anticipated Money, Power, & Sex series and is currently serving as the head screenwriter for the University of Houston HIV Awareness campaign.

Penning the hashtag, #blacklovematters, Norian has been garnering accolades for his work from his reviewers, fans, peers, book clubs, and several podcasts. His books are sold worldwide and are published in print, eBook, and audio formats.

To learn more, visit www.norianlove.com or follow him across most social media outlets at @norianlove.

ALSO BY NORIAN LOVE

Novels
Money, Power & Sex: A Love Story
Seduction: A Money, Power & Sex Story
Autumn: A Love Story

Poetry
Theater of Pain
Games of the Heart
The Dawn or the Dusk
Blue: Love Letters to Fatima

Music
Autumn: The Soundtrack to the Novel

Coming Soon
Marcus: A Money, Power & Sex Novella
Ronnie: A Money, Power & Sex Story
Money, Power & Sex II: The Scent of Deceit
In the Case of Alexandria Hughes

Made in United States
North Haven, CT
20 November 2022